Six Incredibly Interesting Stories

Henry E. Peavler

LIVING SPRINGS PUBLISHERS

Dedicated to Henry E. Peavler, Sr.

Although I barely knew you, other than through
the faded memories of a six-year-old child, some
ancient photographs, and musings of your friends
and family, I've tried my best to live up to the
legacy you left behind. You must have been a
hell of a man, Dad.

Henry E. Peavler Sr. 371st Field Artillery Battery C
99th Infantry Division

Contents

MIDNIGHT CASTLE OF THE GODS

Manny slammed the door, pressed the lock button on the remote, turned and ran toward the front door of the Castle of the Gods with that distinctive jiggle-joggle fat-man gait of those individuals bulky but gracefully athletic. He grasped the door handle, released it, turned and clicked the lock again before entering the building. After clocking in, he stepped back outside and clicked it one last time.

"Manny, why do you have to check it three times?" Billy Wilson, the night clerk asked.

"I didn't. That was only twice, I would never check it three times. The first time was to set it. The second two were to check it. Have you seen Hal?"

"He's upstairs with the Happy Seniors. Why do they call them happy, Manny? They can't be happy as old as they are," Billy's bright red hair spiking in all directions like it had been brushed with an eggbeater, his innocence infuriating in its sincerity.

"Dios Mio, Billy, why would you say such an ignorant thing? I haven't got time to explain it now," Manny ran up the stairs two steps at a time belying his shaking bulk.

Manuel Kelly Gonzales, 38-year-old rotund bundle of energy born of a Mexican mother and an Irish father. Five feet five inches high and wide who looked more like he was rolling than running, entered the large room crammed full of exercise machines, searching frantically for Hal, "I figured it out Hal. I know who stole Bucky's wallet," he shouted across the room.

The Happy Seniors, most standing around visiting, some working out at the simple machines, all stopped to observe the uproar.

"Simple matter of deduction, Hal, I know who it was. It was Ja..."

Hal slapped his hand across Manny's mouth, "I'll be right back Mary. Do another set of four..."

The elderly lady strained to push the mechanical arms together although there was no weight attached. She let out a tennis style yelp causing Hal to wince. He turned around, still stymying Manny's accusation; she batted her eyes, smiled, but didn't make any progress with the machine.

"What the hell, Manny," Hal shushed the raging late night janitor, "you want everyone to think there's a crook loose in here? Keep it down. We'll talk about it later after everyone's gone. I have to get back to help Mary Poppins finish her workout. Go to work and calm down."

Hal Prather, was a 65 year old personal trainer to the old, infirm, deluded, delusional, disillusioned and plain senile. His current client Mary Smith believed that she played Mary Poppins in the movie, The Sound of Music.

"I always thought that Julie Andrews played that part," Hal commented the first time she mentioned it.

"I have heard that malicious rumor before," she said with a quick toss of her silver hair. "I doubt that she was ever even in Lansing, Michigan."

Hal shook his head, accustomed to Mary's non-sequiturs, "Mary, just because the tennis players yell is no reason for a lady of your stature to do it."

"But it helps me with my adrenalin," she smiled her best flirtatious smile.

"Anyway, good job today, you're finished. The bus will be here in about 10 minutes. Everyone from Happy Seniors hit the showers," Hal announced. Several elderly patrons began making their way to the locker rooms. One man in his 80's, small but spry, called to Hal, "Hey youngster come here. You think I can leg press this 100 pounds. You know they called me Whizzer in my day. I played halfback for...."

"I know, Whizzer, you played halfback for the Colorado Buffalos, and you still hold punt return records there but they were lost in a fire and now someone else claims your record. And I do think you can leg press that 100 pounds because I see you do it three times a week.

"Hal, why do you put up with these old farts?"

"I'll tell you why, Whizzer, I am one, that's why I do it."

While waiting for the Happy Seniors to clean up, Hal poked his head into the snack bar. Molly Cartwright, late night snack shop manager, waitress, and cook; skinny, almost anorexic fancies herself a woman of uncommon insight.

"Molly, what's shakin' you lean, mean, fightin' machine?"

"Go bugger yourself, Hal. I've got work to do."

"Bugger? Is that a word, Mol? What is that old English or something? How does one bugger himself anyway?"

"Leave me alone right now; let me make this chocolate malt and cheeseburger for his Majesty. I'll explain it to you later, I'll even watch if you want me to."

"Molly, you're making my heart beat fast. His Majesty hungry again?"

"Yeah, go figure," she laughed reaching for the whipped cream.

"I'll take it, I need to talk to him anyway."

Hal took the snack across the hall to the late-night manager's office. Bif Sparrow was a man of medium height, thinning dark hair combed across his balding forehead and a protruding belly, the result of too many beers and constant eating on the job.

"Bifster, Que paso mi amigo," Hal greeted the manager.

Bif grimaced at the vulgar familiarity but wasted no time on a formal greeting. He was a no-nonsense manager, "Did you find out who took Mr. Goldman's wallet? I suspect one of the colored janitors."

"I have one of my top men on the case, Bify We're close to a breakthrough. Bucky should have his wallet back by tonight. And f.y.i., I don't think it's politically correct to say colored anymore."

"Hal, don't refer to him as Bucky or me as Bify or Bifster or Your Majesty. I've told you a million times to call me mister and show me the respect I deserve."

"Mr. Bify, I've told you a thousand times to quite exaggerating and we call him Bucky to his face. He likes joking around with us. He calls me 'old man' and I don't care. He has an overbite. If he wanted to fix it, he would."

He left Bif fuming at the lack of respect, but Hal knew there was nothing the ineffective manager could do. Hal had a hunch that Goldman left his wallet at home, which would disappoint Manny terribly.

Hal found Manny spraying the shower stalls, "My main Manny, how goes the investigation?"

"Hal, where have you been? Man, I figured it out this morning. It had to be Jarrod."

"Jarrod? Manual Kelly-Gonzales, my favorite Irish Mexican, Jarrod works the day shift. How could he steal a wallet when he was home? And anyway, he would never steal anything."

Manny turned the sprayer off. He went to fetch the large sanitizing bottle, treated his hands and the handle of the sprayer before he continued, "No, listen Hal, LaKesha saw him come in about midnight last night when we were on break. She didn't say anything about it until I called her this afternoon to see if she had seen anything suspicious."

"Really, what was Jarrod doing here at midnight? I saw him when I came on, so I know he was at work today."

"I don't know. Lakesha didn't ask him what he was doing. You know how she is. She chewed me out for thinking it was Jarrod."

"What did she say?"

"She said, 'the first thing you think when there's a crime is the black man did it.' I told her I didn't think about him being black, but didn't it seem suspicious that Jarrod came back at midnight after working all day?"

Manny got a stack of towels and used one to wipe the bench by the shower stalls and used a second one to sit on. There were two men waiting to use the newly cleaned stalls. "Go ahead guys," Manny told them.

"Manny," Hal began tentatively, "have you given any thought to the theory that maybe Bucky left it at home? You know how dramatic he is. Everything is a crisis with him."

"Sure, of course I have, but I think Jarrod took it. Let's go have coffee," Manny placed the towels in the hamper.

Midnight at the Castle of the Gods meant the late-night staff met for coffee in the snack shop. Everyone but Bif Sparrow, who would dawdle around the Whey Protein poster checking to see if they were talking about him. They sat around the large round table near the snack shop entrance so they could watch the comings and goings.

"How's Clarence's new job?" Molly asked Lakesha, a stout lady with dark intelligent eyes, hair piled on top of her head and the dusky skin tone of a rich cup of coffee.

"What new job?" she looked askance at Molly.

"Clarence told George that he had a new job." Clarence was Lakesha's son who lived in her basement and was pretty much a deadbeat as was George, Molly's son, for that matter.

The lady's custodian scoffed, "That boy wouldn't know how to spell job if you spotted him the j and the o. When did he tell George that he had a job?"

"I don't know, maybe Monday."

"I haven't seen him come out of the basement in three days. I doubt there are many jobs that pay you to smoke weed, drink booze and sleep all day?"

"Kesh, why do you put up with him?" Billy asked, "Why don't you just kick him out?"

LaKesha glared at Billy, which always intimidated him, but it didn't take much to intimidate the young night clerk. "Billy, until you have kids of your own don't be givin' advice. He's my son and the father of my grandchildren and if I kick him out he'll take the kids with him. Now don't tell me that he won't because you don't know that," she cautioned all of them.

"Lakesha, you have a heart of gold," Hal said.

Billy hurried to change to subject hoping to deflect Lakesha's scorn, "Did Jarrod steal a wallet?"

"Jarrod stole a wallet?" Molly scoffed, "Are you kidding me? No way he did. What makes you say that?"

"He's black ain't he?" Lakesha crossed her arms and glared at Manny.

"Nobody is accusing anyone of anything," Hal also glared at him.

"Whizzer told me that Jarrod stole Mr. Goldman's wallet," Billy smiled proudly.

"What?" Manny held up his hands, "I swear, I didn't mention any names."

"Is that the truth? I don't understand what's going on here," Molly slammed her cup down.

"You won't understand the truth," Billy said trying to imitate Jack Nicholson.

"No, Billy, it's not *understand* the truth. It's 'You can't handle the truth.'" Manny corrected him angrily, "Have you even seen the movie? Dame fuerza!"

"What movie?" Billy smiled innocently.

Molly slapped the table, "Ok, it doesn't matter about the stupid movie. Who is accusing Jarrod of stealing a wallet because he's a good kid and wouldn't steal anything."

"Hey, look who just came in," Billy pointed at the entrance.

They turned in unison to watch Mike (Bucky) Goldman stroll in. Bucky, in his fifties, still showed signs of an athletic past. He reached over the counter to swipe his membership card in the card reader; standard procedure when no one was at the desk. Goldman spotted the night crew in the snack bar, "What's happening guys? Hey, old man, you got time to play some racquetball?"

They all stared at him.

"Yeah, Bucky, sure. I've got a 20-minute demonstration to a new member first. We were just talking about you."

"Really, what?"

"Your wallet."

"My...? Oh yeah, I left it in the car. I found it last night when I got home. I'll see you at the courts in half an hour, ok?" Bucky hurried off to the locker room leaving the five friends to their thoughts.

"Well, Hell," Manny pushed his chair back.

"Like they say, gossip is half right and part wrong," Billy returned his cup to the kitchen.

"What? Half right and part wrong? Where do you come up with this crap?" Manny shook his head incredulously watching Billy walk back to the reception desk.

"Hal, why do they call them Happy Seniors?"

"That's just the name of the place they live." Hal hurried off to walk with Manny before Billy could say more.

"Good thing you didn't say anything to Jarrod," Hal put his arm around Manny as they walked back to the locker room. Manny didn't answer.

"Manny, you didn't say anything did you?"

"Not to Jarrod."

Hal stopped and looked at his friend. Manny wouldn't look at him.

"Who Manny?" Hal asked, "Who did you tell?"

"Bifster."

Hal turned and ran down the hall. The insecure Manager would move quickly on this newfound false information. Bif wanted to do something to prove to the Owner that he is capable, not inept; a difficult task given that he is inept. Jarrod walked out of the office as Hal opened the door, Bif right behind him. Jarod was taller than Hal, a gangly, youthful man of 21 bout to enter law school. He worked at the Castle to pay back his mother who put him through college without getting a student loan.

"Hal, that fool just fired me. Said I stole Bucky's wallet. I didn't steal a wallet."

"I know you didn't Jarrod, just wait a minute. It was a mistake, Bif, Jarrod didn't steal anything. Bucky found his wallet in his car. He didn't tell us about it until tonight. So, let's apologize to Jarrod and everything is back to normal."

"Well, not so fast," Bif growled, his face red, spittle shooting from his lips, "I just fired him. He was insubordinate, called me a fool, said he was going to sue me. I can't allow that kind of insubordination. No sir, he is fired and that's that." Bif stalked back and forth while Hal and Jarrod watched.

"Bif, be reasonable. It was a mistake," Hal repeated.

"Reasonable? I said he was fired and that's that, Goddamnit. I'm the boss here not you Prather. I said this boy is fired and that's the way it is. Now get out."

"Boy?" Jarrod said glaring down at the smaller man, "What the hell do the men look like where you come from you ignorant cracker?"

Hal pulled Jarrod into the hall, "You aren't fired be back here at your regular time and go to work tomorrow. I'll take care of this and I am sorry about everything, Jarrod. It should never have happened."

"Ok, Hal, you've never led me wrong, but what is up with that guy, did his momma drop him on his head when he was little?"

"The truth is he's the Big Guy's brother-in-law, but he doesn't want anyone to know about it. Believe me that's the only reason he's working here. His wife is the owner's sister. Be here tomorrow and go to work. See you then, Jarrod; and again, I am sorry about this."

Hal bolted up the stairs two at a time to meet his new client at the trainer's desk. The woman weighed three hundred pounds and was breathing heavily from her own trip up the stairs.

"I should have taken the elevator," she tried to catch her breath.

Hal took her vital signs, asked the required waiver questions about health and exercise habits, what she did for a living and her diet. Obviously, it would be a challenge. He hoped she would have the stamina and desire to stick with the program he envisioned.

"We're going to start out really slow, Mrs. Thompson."

"I think the walk up the stairs is enough for today," she put her hands on her knees gasping for air.

Mrs. Thompson mounted the treadmill for her stress test and began walking as slow as the machine would allow. She gripped the rail tightly. The machine was barely moving.

"Hi Hal," announced a newly arrived couple the staff called Ken and Barbie, part of the body building clique.

"Is that his wife?" Mrs. Thompson asked, "I heard that she's pregnant."

"I've always assumed it's his wife. Why? Do you know them?"

"I know who he is. Larry Vandergrift, his father's a State Senator and they own the First United Bank. I've never seen his wife, but I heard about how beautiful she is."

"Really!" Hal exclaimed. He was excited about this bit of gossip, something new to share with the staff at their next coffee break. The body-builder clique was notorious for their snobbish ways. At least as far as the staff was concerned.

"They think they're better than us," Molly sat down as Hal announced the new piece of gossip from Mrs. Thompson.

"Not all of them," Hal responded, "most of them say 'Hi' at least."

"Not to me," Lakesha said.

"They act like I'm invisible," Billy replied.

"Do you say anything to them, Billy?" Manny asked.

"I always say, 'welcome to the Castle of the Gods.'"

"Billy, if you see them every night you don't say that. Only say that to people you don't know. If you know them just say hi or hello. They'll think you're retarded if you say that every time they come in," Lakesha lectured.

"Yeah!" Molly agreed. "Plus, you see their name on the screen when you check them in. Say hello and their name."

"I'll try but they just don't like me. I can tell."

Hal wrestled with what to do about the Jarrod situation. Bif would be angry when Jarrod arrived at work in the morning. Hal announced his plan to the group and coached them on what to say. It wasn't long before Bif was spotted spying from behind the electronic stopwatch display.

"Now," Hal whispered.

They began hugging each other and crying, making a show of gathering their personal belongings then started toward the door.

"I'll stop and tell Bifster," Hal announced sadly. "I'm going to miss all of you. It's been a great run here at the Castle."

"Thanks for everything, Hal." Manny sobbed, over-acting like a character in a bad movie. Hal was afraid Manny was going to fling himself to the ground.

Bif stepped out as if he were just passing by, "What's happening here? Where are you going?"

"You should know, you caused it," Molly sobbed.

"Because of you we don't have jobs anymore," Manny wailed and gestured as if he were going to grab the startled manager.

"What the hell are you talking about?" Bif began to get angry.

"You're in trouble now," Lakesha pointed her finger at him, "Jarrod's uncle is gonna' sue you. I hate to be in your shoes when the Big Guy finds out."

"I wish I was gonna be there to see it." Molly wailed. "You deserve to go to jail for what you did."

"Now just a minute. What's this all about, Prather?" Bif looked at Hal.

"It's simple, you fired Jarrod and now his famous uncle is going to sue you and the Big Guy for everything, including this building."

"He can't do that. I had just cause."

"No you didn't," Manny countered. "Jarrod didn't do it. We told you that, but you fired him anyway. Now his uncle is on his way to see the Big Guy. I'd hate to be in your shoes in about four hours when the Big Guy hears what you did."

"Well, who's this famous uncle you're talking about?"

"Just Johnny Cochran, the most famous attorney in California. He got O.J. Simpson off. Think what he'll do to you,"

"What are you talking about? He's dead."

"The old man is but not his son. He's even better than his dad was," Hal said. "They already have the writs and motions and court orders ready to go. They're headed to the Big Guy's house at 8 in the morning."

Bif began to sweat and his wispy hair fell into his eyes. He glanced nervously from person to person looking for an ally, "But that isn't the way it happened. The Big Guy'll understand when he hears the truth."

Billy shouted, "You can't handle the truth," then glanced at Manny with a big grin on his face.

"What?" Bif's resolve began to waver, "Look Prather, maybe I was a little hasty. I really didn't mean that he was permanently fired. I just meant a temporary layoff. He can come back to work next week."

"Tell it to the Judge," Manny screamed.

"I don't even know if I can get him to come back now, Bifster. His attorneys have him convinced that he can end up owning this place."

"Yeah, that's right," Lakesha hit him on the shoulder with her purse. "Slave days is over, Master Manager."

"All of you go back to work. Jarrod isn't fired. All he has to do is apologize to me in the morning when he comes to work."

"I might be able to get him to come back if you apologize to him in the morning," Hal countered.

Bif glared at him then yelled, "Fine, I'll do it. Now go back to work all of you. Molly bring me a cheeseburger and some fries and a chocolate milk shake. Jesus Christ, what has this world come to?" He slammed the door to his office as the staff began laughing and high fiving each other.

Having resolved the situation with Jarrod, Hal strolled through the building watching the various people in their routines. A group of Muslim women were in the swimming pool, their bodies covered from head to foot. The bodybuilders were in the free weight room. Hal stopped and watched. He observed Ken and Barbie spotting each other at the bench press station.

"Anything I can help with," Hal asked.

"No, we're fine. Thanks, though," Barbie answered with a sincere smile.

Hal wanted to visit and gather more gossip for the staff gossip session later.

"Would you explain this machine to me, Hal? Pretty please," Mrs. Kirby asked. Hal was enamored of the beautiful woman who came to work out every other day at three in the morning. She had never asked him for help before.

"Sure Mrs. Kirby, I'll be glad to."

"Please, Hal, call be Barbara."

"Ok, Barbara," He began to explain the new rowing machine with the complicated control system. "How is Mr. Kirby? I don't recall if he ever comes to workout with you."

"I've been divorced for years. I thought you knew that," she said with a surprised look.

"I did not, but I wish that I would have. I'm divorced too."

"Isn't that a coincidence? Maybe we could have a cup of coffee and discuss it after my workout."

"What a great idea. In the coffee shop at say six?"

"Perfect, that gives me time to finish and take a shower. See you later. Thanks for the instruction, Hal."

Hal rushed down to the locker room to share the news with Manny. He was so excited he almost ran into Ken and Barbie who were arguing fiercely as they left the gym. Hal followed them trying to hear what they were saying. He overheard Barbie say that whatever she was angry about she would not allow Ken to get away with it. Lakesha was cleaning near the entrance to the snack shop as the pair stormed out the door.

"You hear that?" she pointed with her dust mop.

"I sure did. What do you think it was about?"

"I don't know but he be on the couch tonight," she laughed. Hal shook his head and remembered the good news about Mrs. Kirby flirting with him.

"I've got a coffee date with Mrs. Kirby at six, Kesh."

"Ooooh, she's a pretty one. Better not let Bifster find out you're fraternizing."

Lakesha laughed as Hal ran, almost skipping, to share with Manny.

"What did she say exactly?" Manny pounded his friend on the back almost as excited as Hal.

"Well, she said that she was divorced, and she thought I already knew that she was. Then when I said that I was divorced she said we should get together in the coffee shop to discuss it. Then I said how about six and she agreed. So, we're meeting at six for coffee," Hal recounted eagerly.

"Sounds like she has the hots for you, Hal. Maybe you'll finally get laid again."

"Thanks a lot, Manny. That isn't very nice, you've got Maria at home waiting for you."

"You've had plenty of chances, Hal. Now don't screw this up. Mrs. Kirby is a class act."

"Barbara," Hal corrected him.

"Hurra, amigo, already on a first name basis. Bifster isn't going to like you socializing with the customers."

"He'll be laying low for a few days after this thing with Jarrod. By the way, did Ken come in here? I saw him and Barbie arguing in the lobby, and they were pretty mad at each other."

"Yeah, he grabbed his gym bag and slammed the locker shut. He stormed out of here and didn't even say goodbye to his buddies. They laughed. One of them said, uh oh, looks like trouble in paradise."

Hal gave him a hand folding towels as they talked. Lakesha joined them standing in the attendant's booth located between the entrance to the men's and women's locker room. Gathering, washing and folding towels was a never-ending job at Castle of the God's. The day crew had a special attendant who spent all her time working on that one job. But at night Lakesha and Manny were responsible.

"Well, I doubt if we'll ever know what it was about. I'll bet they come back tomorrow night just like nothing ever happened."

"I'd sure like to play kiss and make up with her," Manny said.

"In your dreams Manuel Kelly-Gonzales," Kesh snapped him with a towel. "You best watch out; I'll see Maria tomorrow. What do you think she's gonna' say when she hears about that kind of talk."

At five the night shift clocked out and the morning shift took over. Hal changed his Castle of the God's uniform for a nice sports shirt and a pair of jeans. He brushed his teeth and combed his grey hair, stared at his reflection for a while and contemplated where the years had gone. Most 65-year-old men would do about anything to be as fit as he, but all Hal could think about were the lines in his face and the droop in his eyelids. Barbara was probably shy of 50. He suddenly had doubts about starting another relationship. He took a deep breath and convinced himself that it was nothing more than a conversation with a new friend.

Barbara was waiting with cups of coffee when he arrived, "I asked Molly how you liked your coffee, and she whipped it up before she left. I hope that's what you wanted, Hal."

"Molly makes it just the way I like it with honey instead of sugar. How was your workout?"

"Pretty good. I like the new rowing machine. Especially after I got the hang of it. You're so fit you must work out every day."

"I used to but now I just work out with whoever my clients are. As I get older I find that doing more weights and less cardio works better...I'm 65," Hal blurted out then regretted being so abrupt. He watched her closely for a negative reaction.

"I know. I asked Lakesha how old you are."

"Really, when did you do that?"

"I don't know exactly. Sometime last week."

"I'm surprised Kesh didn't say something to me. She loves stuff like that."

"She told Molly because when I asked her to make the coffee, she said that Lakesha told her that I liked you."

Hal choked on his coffee. After wiping his chin with the napkin, he finally asked, "Do you?"

"Maybe. I don't really know yet. But I'd like to find out. You're a little hesitant because you've been looking at me for a month but never said anything."

"I thought that you were married. Everyone calls you Mrs. Kirby so I just assumed that there was a Mr. Kirby. Now that I know different and especially since Molly and Lakesha have let the cat out of the bag that you like me, I'll change my behavior. Would you like to have dinner with me Friday night, Mrs. Kirby?"

Barbara put her head back in a full-throated delightful laugh, "Well, first you ignore me for a month then you ask for a date before we finish our coffee."

"I'm afraid my relationship skills are a little rusty. But will you go?"

"I'd love to Mr. Prather. What time and where?"

The next shift topic of conversation was, of course, Hal and Barbara's upcoming date. Each of the staff had a recommendation for where they should go. Billy suggested bowling and hamburgers at the Bowl-Inn. Manny lobbied for an all you can eat buffet and a movie. Lakesha and Molly won with their suggestion of the swanky Englishmen's Restaurant and Pub.

"Just sit and talk a while," Lakesha counseled. "Have a couple of drinks and loosen up. You're tighter than a drum you're so nervous," she giggled.

"No, I'm not, Kesha. I still remember how to do this."

"I doubt it," Molly placed his coffee on the table. "It took you a month to even ask her out."

"I thought she was married," Hal was getting a little defensive.

"I've got some more news," Lakesha announced. "Barbie ain't Ken's wife."

"What do you mean, Kesh?" Manny's eyes lit up. A new mystery?

"I saw Ken and his wife at the clinic over on Main and his wife is big old pregnant and it ain't Barbie. They were all lovey-dovey and he was rubbin' her tummy and carryin' on."

"Mrs. Thompson said that she thought Ken's wife was pregnant." Hal reminded them.

"Then who is Barbie," Billy asked?

"I guess his girlfriend," Molly suggested.

The front door flew open and Ken charged in, stopped as he passed the attendant's desk forgetting to swipe his card. He ran back and passed it under the reader then rushed toward the locker room. When he saw the staff, he hesitated in surprise and slowed down, tried to act normal. He waved tentatively at them sporting a half-hearted smile, "Hey everyone, how are you?"

His white t-shirt was stained red and soaking wet, as was his hair. When he passed the door to the snack bar, he started running to the locker room, his gym bag in hand. They all turned to watch until he disappeared around the corner.

"What the hell was that about?" Manny turned back to the group.

"He looked like he hurt himself," Molly said.

"More like he hurt someone else," Lakesha said to Manny.

Manny nodded, "I agree, something big is going on. Someone needs to go find out."

"Yeah," Billy agreed, as they all turned to Hal.

Hal turned toward the large Bird of Paradise plant where Bif was pretending to check the leaves for fungus, "Bif go check on Ken. He looked like he was hurt."

"Not me, don't you know who his family is? And don't call him Ken, I don't want to make them mad," Bif hurried back to his office.

Hal turned to Manny, "Come on then. I'm not going by myself."

They jogged into the hall following the mysterious body builder. When they reached the men's locker room Ken came rushing out, brushed past them with a "Hi Fella's."

Hal and Manny watched as he bounded up the stairs wearing a clean yellow t-shirt with the slogan 'Marriage isn't a word. It's a sentence' printed on the back.

The next night the mystery deepened when Ken returned to the gym again without Barbie.

"I don't know what to think. Have any of you seen her around town or anywhere else?" Molly asked.

"I haven't," Lakesha shook her head, "but I talked to my sister, she's a nurse at the clinic, and she said that Ken and his wife are in there all the time and they seem real happy."

"I went through the trash looking for the blood-stained shirt he was wearing but he must have put it back in his gym bag," Manny explained.

Hal stirred honey into his coffee, "I don't know what to think either but there must be a good explanation for it all."

"Yeah, there's an explanation. He murdered her and got rid of the evidence before his wife finds out," Lakesha said.

"And she was such a nice girl. Always had a kind word for me," Billy sniffled, putting his face in his hands. The red hair radiating like tentacles on an octopus.

"Billy, you're full of it. She never said a word to you," Molly scoffed.

Hal cautioned, "Don't get all carried away. I promise you there's a logical explanation to all of this. We'll laugh at ourselves when she comes back."

"Don't be so sure, Hal. Rich playboy, son of a Senator, with a pregnant wife and girlfriend that's a ball and chain around his neck. Stranger things have happened," Manny shook his finger for emphasis.

"Yeah, Hal, truth and fiction are really strange," Billy chimed in.

Everyone looked at him. Finally, Molly admonished, "Billy, please, just be quiet. This is a serious discussion."

"I was being serious. Isn't that how it goes?"

"It goes, 'Truth is stranger than fiction," Manny said patiently.

"Ok, it doesn't matter. Stay focused here. We've got a crime to report," Lakesha reached for her phone.

"Whoa, hold on. What crime? Report to who? We don't even know if anything has happened," Hal stood up.

"Why don't you just go talk to him," Billy asked?

"Oh yeah, that's a great idea. Go ask the Senator's son, Say Ken, ole buddy ole pal, did you murder your girlfriend?" Manny mimicked.

"Well, you don't say it like that," Billy had a hurt tone in his voice.

"Maybe Billy's on to something," Lakesha agreed. "Maybe Hal should just go and talk to him general like... ask him where Barbie is."

"That's not a bad idea," Molly agreed.

"What's Barbie's real name," Hal asked?

They all turned to Billy who looked away disinterested, "Oh, I thought she never spoke to me. How would I know her name?"

"Come on Billy, this is serious."

"Her real name is Theresa and her last name is Vandergrift and Ken's name is Larry Vandergrift."

"He married two women," Lakesha nodded perceptively.

"He's a bigamist," Molly agreed.

"Maybe he's a Mormon." Manny volunteered.

"More probably she's his sister," Hal said.

"I'll bet that's it. Go find out Hal," Lakesha said. "Just walk by him nonchalant and ask him why Theresa hasn't been in."

Hal left the snack shop intent on checking about Ken but first he had an appointment with the Happy Seniors. The patrons from the retirement home were already on the treadmills and bikes when Hal arrived. They were a fun-loving group but serious about their fitness. These were the ambulatory patients who could get around on their own. Hal traveled twice a week to their facility and conducted fitness classes for those in wheelchairs and walkers. He loved working with the spry, funny group of people.

"Hey youngster," Whizzer called to Hal, "what do you think about Mary?"

"What do you mean, Whizzer? What do I think about her? I think she's a nice lady."

"Not a bad looker either, huh? What do you think?"

"Are you interested in her romantically?"

"You think I'm too old?"

"No not at all. I guess I hadn't thought about it. Have you talked to her? Asked her for a date?"

"No but I think I will."

"When?"

"No time like the present," Whizzer walked confidently toward Mary who was talking with one of her friends while they rode stationary bikes. Hal followed along discreetly.

"Hey Mary, what's shaking with you," he leaned against the handlebars of her bike. He was shorter than Mary with an impish twinkle in his blue eyes. His bald head gleamed in the harsh lights of the gym but he turned on his brightest smile.

Mary was obviously surprised and took a moment to respond. Finally, she looked at her friend, shook her silver hair and replied haughtily, "I'm quite positive I don't have any idea what you mean, Charles."

"Everyone calls me Whizzer because I was a halfback on the Colorado Buffalos football team," he informed her with athletic dignity.

"Well, I'm certain that I shall never address you by that vulgar name. Now what is it you want?"

"There's a Cary Grant movie on tomorrow night and I would like you to attend the show with me."

"I was a particular favorite of Cary's you know. He wanted me to play the part that Eva Marie Saint took... stole from me by... well, I won't even mention what methods she used to get that part and deprive me of another starring role. Cary was heartbroken as I'm sure you are aware."

Whizzer stood quietly confused, not sure what to say. He looked to Hal for help.

Hal hurried over, "I suppose that means you will go to the movie with Whiz...uh, Charles, right Mary?"

Mary's friend on the adjoining bike giggled, "Oh go ahead, Mary. The old coot looks harmless enough."

"I doubt that you even know Cecil B. DeMille," Mary glared at Whizzer.

"No, Mary, I'm sorry to say I don't."

"Ok, I'll go." She said with finality and turned back to her friend. Whizzer smiled broadly, placed himself between the two ladies and joined enthusiastically in their conversation. Hal wondered off shaking his head. He walked into the weight room where Ken and several of his friends were lifting. Stray towels were lying around so Hal began picking them up.

"Hey Prather," one of the younger men said with a sneer, "can't you keep these weights in the right place? People keep leaving them out. It's your job to keep this place cleaned up. It looks like a pig sty."

It got quiet in the room as Hal turned toward the arrogant young body builder and said with a military tone in his voice, "You put those weights back in the rack. I believe you're the one who used them."

The two stared at each other. Hal was comfortable with the reputation he had of being an x-green beret with a mean streak. A rumor that Billy and Manny spread among the staff and clients, and no matter how many times Hal downplayed it, the more the legend grew.

Finally, Larry walked over to his friend, "Come on Barry, you asshole, you did use them. Put them back." The young man seemed relieved and went about the task without any further incident giving Hal an opening to question them, "Thanks, Larry. By the way, where's Theresa been lately? Haven't seen her around in a while."

"She went to Phoenix, to visit my sister. She'll be back next week."

Hal blurted out, "I thought she was your sister."

Larry laughed. "Everyone thinks that. But she's my mom."

"Your mom? Wow that surprises the hell out of me."

"Yeah, it does everybody. She had me when she was 18. She's 40 but looks like she's 30."

"Twenty," one of his friends said.

"Watch it," Larry warned him. The subject must have come up before.

Hal hurried to find Lakesha to share this new information.

"His Mom? Yeah, right, maybe I'm his aunt," Lakesha scoffed when Hal told her the news.

"I believe him Kesh. Let's wait and see if she does come back next week like he says. Nothing else we can do anyway. Say, have you seen Jarrod? He didn't come to work today according to Manny."

"No, it ain't my day to keep track of that boy. Go ask his Majesty if he came today. He keeps track of him, I promise."

Hal went straight to Bif's office. "Did you apologize to Jarrod?"

"Didn't get the chance. He came in here and said he was quitting. Told me to send his last check to his mom and gave me the address."

"Why didn't you tell anyone?"

"I'm the damn manager here, Prather, not you. I don't have to tell you what goes on here. I'm in charge."

"Well, I'll tell you this, Bify. If I find out he quit because of something you did, you'll have a lot more to worry about than if you're in charge or not."

"Are you threatening me?"

"Yes, absolutely! And it's not a threat. It's a fact! You think you don't want Larry Vandergrift's people mad at you. Wait until you see my friends. No, check that, Mister Bifster, you won't see them, but they'll see you."

The manager glared at Hal as he stalked out the door. He found Lakesha just going into the lady's locker room, "Kesh, wait a minute. Can you call Jarrod's mom and find out what's going on? Bif says that Jarrod quit yesterday. Do you know anything about it?"

"No, but I'll find out and let you know."

Hal went to the snack bar and sat down with a splitting headache. It was Friday and he had a date with Barbara Kirby for six. He needed to go to the grocery store, the bank and get a haircut. Plus, he really needed to work some sleep into his schedule sometime.

"Having a bad day, Hal," Molly asked?

"No, not really, Molly. How about you? Everything going ok?"

"Well, my son, George, got his second DUI and my dead-beat ex won't do anything to help. My boyfriend is drunk on the couch waiting for me to come home and make him breakfast. I'd say everything is just normal as hell," she laughed.

Hal smiled at her and shook his head. "I guess I better get back to work. It's almost quittin' time, isn't it?"

"One hour Hal. Enjoy your date with Mrs. Kirby tonight."

The evening started a bit slow for both Hal and Barbara. The Englishman's Pub tried hard to be authentic but came up a little short resulting in an atmosphere more old LA than old London. But the drinks were good and the waitress enthusiastic. Hal was dressed in a sports shirt with grey slacks and a blue blazer. Barbara wore a close-fitting blue skirt that ended well above her knees. Her well-toned body was the object of many side glances from the others at the restaurant. After the first drink they both loosened up a bit.

"I know a lot about you, Hal. Probably more than you want me to know. I thought I'd tell you up front so that we start out even."

"How do you know it's the truth? Whatever it is you've found out about me?"

"I know Mel Garrett well. My ex and I were good friends with him and Linda."

"How is the Colonel? I haven't talked to him in a long time."

"He seems to be getting along well. Exceptionally well for someone who's 85 years old. He speaks very highly of you."

"Hard to believe he's that old but he seemed old to me when we were in Vietnam together. What did he tell you about me?"

"Why don't you tell me the story and then I'll compare it with what he said."

"Not much to tell, Barbara. I got out of high school and went into the Army. Served two tours in Vietnam the last one under the Colonel. Of course, he was a Lieutenant then. Got out of the service and went to Stanford on the GI Bill. Got out of college and went into the Insurance business. Made a lot of money and retired five years ago when my wife and I divorced. The kids are all grown, families of their own, so I went to work at the Castle to have something to do. That's about it."

Barbra laughed shaking her head, "Typical man, you give the basics but leave out the details. Let's see if I can remember all of it. High school football star, purple heart hero in Vietnam, all American tight end at Stanford, married with three children and five grandchildren, wrote two books still used in the Insurance Industry as training manuals, retired at 60 with more money than you can possibly spend and now you work as a Personal Fitness trainer at a fitness club."

"That's pretty close to what I said. Tell me about yourself."

The evening was the most pleasant Hal could remember in the past five years. He had forgotten how enjoyable it was to have a woman laugh at a joke and how relaxing to share intimate conversation together. When the meal came, they talked between bites sharing stories of their children and grandchildren. The clinking of glasses, conversation from adjoining tables and the bustle of the waiters faded into the old wood paneling and the couple felt that it was just the two of them sharing a private dinner at home.

Before they knew it time had passed to where Hal needed to leave for work.

"How about a movie tomorrow night? I'm off on the weekends and won't have a curfew."

"Well, maybe I have a curfew, Mr. Prather. What did you have in mind that would require staying out so late?'"

"I may be old and grey, Barbara, but I haven't forgotten everything."

"You really are trying to make up for lost time. To answer your question, I'd be delighted to go to a movie with you. I haven't been to one in a long time."

"Shall I pick you up at six again? We'll have dinner at the theater."

Hal was exhilarated from the excitement of the evening with Barbara. He arrived at work ten minutes late still wearing the clothes from his date, planning to change at the club. It was evident something was up as soon as he walked in the door. Billy began shouting into his radio, "Hal is here. He's here Manny. I'll send him down. Where have you been, Hal? We've been looking all over for you. Get down to the storage room right now. Manny needs you."

"Ok, Billy, calm down. What's up?"

"I'm not sure but Manny and Lakesha found something. Hurry they're really worried."

Molly intercepted Hal as he walked by the snack bar. She whispered to him urgently, "Shall I call the police now or wait."

Hal was startled but managed to say, "Wait, I don't even know what's going on."

Her comment caused him to break into a trot down the hall and into the storage room just inside the entrance to the men's locker room. The door to the storage room was in the crook of an L-shaped hall which allowed both the men and women employees to gain entrance without bothering the men in the locker room. Manny and Lakesha urged him inside and closed the door. Manny pointed to something behind one of the storage shelves at ground level, uncovered when the large box on the bottom shelf had been moved. The object was a white, blood-stained t-shirt.

"I found it when I was lookin' for some paper towels," Lakesha said. "I moved that big box and there it was. He stuck it back there thinkin' nobody would ever find it."

"We've got to call the police now," Manny bounced around with nervous excitement.

Hal was studying the situation with a great deal more caution than his colleagues, "Have you touched anything?"

"Of course not, I've seen every cop show ever made. We got to photograph everything and get a plastic bag to put the evidence in," Lakesha was almost as nervous as Manny.

"Just a minute you guys. Look at this logically. I don't think he was trying to hide it. I think he was trying to throw it into the big trash barrel there next to the shelves and he missed, and it slipped down behind that big carton. Think about it. The closest trash can is on the way out of the locker room entrance but he walks by here and sees this door is open so he just tosses it toward that trash can and misses."

Lakesha and Manny look at each other. Then begin talking at once chastising Hal.

"What difference does it make why it's here? The Police gonna' want to see it no matter how it got here," Lakesha said.

"Hal, you can't protect the guy now. We know he did it."

"Did what? There isn't a crime. We've been over this."

"Didn't you read the paper today?" Lakesha admonished him.

"No, I had a bunch of errands, then I slept until my date with Barbara. Why, what are you talking about?

"I left a message on your phone."

"My phone has been off since I went to sleep. What's going on?"

Lakesha pulled a well folded newspaper article from her pocket and handed it to Hal. The headline read, 'Local Student Missing.'

'A 19-year-old student at Grimes County Junior College has been reported missing. Leslie Ann Stallings was last seen Wednesday evening as she left her apartment telling her room-mate she would be back later that night. Her mother, Mary Stallings reports that she believed, from a note found in Leslie Ann's bedroom, that she was meeting someone at the 24-hour fitness center known as Castle of the Gods.'

The article described a few other details, but Hal stopped at that point, "Alright, leave everything as it is and lock this door right now. Don't go back in there until we straighten this out, ok?"

Manny's radio crackled. Billy's voice sounded frantic, "Manny, Hal doesn't answer my call. There's some lady here to see him. She's crying. He needs to come now. I don't know what to do."

"Tell him I'm on my way."

Hal ran back up the hall to see about the new crisis. He hoped that no one had been hurt. The entire staff was trained in what to do in a medical emergency, but they all preferred to call him when there was a problem. A middle-aged lady sat in the alcove where the television was tuned to ESPN. Her eyes were red. She obviously hadn't slept in a long while.

"May I help you," Hal reached to shake her hand.

"Are you Mr. Prather," she dabbed at her eyes with a tissue?

"Yes."

"My name is Mary Stallings. I spoke with the owner, Mr. Goldman, and he told me to contact you. I asked him if he could help but he told me not to speak with anyone but you. It's about my missing daughter."

"I just found out about the situation Mrs. Stallings. I'm very sorry but I don't know that I can help you. You should go to the police."

"I've been to the police, but they won't help. They think she's run off with a boyfriend or something. The police talked to your boss, and he told them to talk to you. I thought they would have been here by now. They say there isn't any evidence of a crime being committed. I'm at my wits end. I don't know where to turn. I thought I would come here and see if I could find out anything."

"Do you have a picture?" Hal asked.

She pulled a picture from an envelope. A six by eight portrait, probably her high school senior picture, a pretty girl with a typical blonde California look about her. She could have been anyone's daughter. Not particularly someone who stood out.

"I don't know her," Hal looked carefully, "but, if you can leave this picture I'll ask around and see if anyone recognizes her. Why do you think she came here?"

"I found this in her room." She handed Hal a copy of a note which had been pasted together from pieces pulled from the trash. Obviously not all the pieces had been found. The note said Midni...Cast of the Go...arr. " It says Midnight Castle of the Gods and a name. But I can't make out the name. The first and last letters are smudged."

Hal's heart sank as he realized that it was Larry's name. He needed to discuss it with the others. But first he tried to console Mrs. Stallings. The decision not to tell her anything was difficult yet necessary. He told her he would get back with her in the morning after he had quizzed the staff and as many clients as he could. The thought of calling the police was beginning to sound more and more likely. Hal prided himself on his judgement and just couldn't bring himself to believe that Larry had killed anyone. But the evidence was incriminating. If he waited any longer, he would be negligent. On the other hand, if they were wrong about Larry the consequences would be severe both for the young man and for the Castle of the Gods.

"Do you know if she was dating anyone?"

"Not that I know of. Her roommate told me she was seeing someone but didn't know who it was. Leslie and I haven't been on good terms for a few weeks. She felt that I was prying into her affairs. I tried to back off, but she always returned my phone calls. This is not like her at all. I haven't talked to her in almost three days."

"So, it is possible that she went somewhere with someone?"

"I suppose so but why won't she answer my calls and why did she tell her roommate she would be back that night?"

Larry and his friends walked through the lobby on their way to the weight room.

Mrs. Stallings pointed, "I know those boys. They went to school with Leslie Ann. Maybe they know something. That tall blond boy is Larry Vandergrift and the shorter one is Barry Johnson. Hey, Larry, could I speak to you for a minute," she shouted.

"Mrs. Stallings, we heard about Leslie. Have you found out anything?"

"No, do you boys know anything that might help me?" She began crying harder and the boys were visibly upset."

"I haven't talked to her since high school. Have any of you guys?"

"I see her around campus now and then over at Grimes, but we just say hi," one of the other boys answered.

Larry put his hand on her shoulder, "I'm sure she's fine, Mrs. Stallings. But I'll ask around to see if anyone knows anything." The boys were uncomfortable and didn't know what else to say. They wandered off toward the locker rooms.

"There are two boys whose names would fit," she said.

"Why don't you go back to the police and tell them about this Mrs. Stallings. That might get them to move a little faster. But the boys denied knowing anything."

Hal couldn't think of any further questions but began to have doubts that foul play was involved. He understood why the police were hesitant to call it a crime yet. Of course, Hal's co-workers wouldn't accept that as an answer.

"What you mean you don't think there's been a crime?" Lakesha asked him angrily. Her dark eyes scowled with indignation. She crossed her arms; they all knew to tread lightly.

Manny supported Lakesha's point of view even going so far as to pound his fist on the table, "Come on Hal. How can you ignore the evidence? It's all right there. Anyone can tell what happened. He killed his girlfriend to hide it from his wife. It's just a different girlfriend from the one we thought it was."

"Well, it doesn't feel right to me. I'm going to go and talk to him and see why his t-shirt had blood on it that night."

They all spoke at once telling him what a fool he was to do that.

"It's a police matter now," Molly insisted.

Lakesha's phone rang while they were arguing with Hal. "Be quiet, its Bertha, Jarrod's momma." Lakesha left the group and went into the kitchen to answer the call because the others were loudly telling Hal to call the police.

When LaKesha returned she was visibly upset. "Bertha says Jarrod has been actin' crazy since he got fired. I said he wasn't fired it was a misunderstanding. Bertha says that something is wrong with Jarrod cause he missed school and that ain't like him."

"Call Bertha back and tell her to have Jarrod call me. He won't answer my calls either," Hal furrowed his brow, "I need to talk to him and see if Bif caused him to act that way. Damnit, why does Jarrod have to do this now when all this other mess is going on?" Hal said.

Barry and Larry kept running through Hal's mind as Lakesha and Manny continued lobbying for calling the police. Barry was the more likely suspect, but the bloody t-shirt couldn't be ignored. He was going to go and talk to Larry about it whether the others wanted him to or not.

"Hey Larry, how's the workout tonight," Hal asked?

"Not good, Hal. All of us are worried about Leslie. I didn't know her that well, but Barry did. You dated her for a while didn't you Barry?"

"Not really dated. We were on the debate team together. That was about it."

Hal couldn't picture the arrogant little prick being on the debate team. But he didn't want to let his anger at the boy color his thinking. He was beginning to like Barry more and more as the prime suspect. He started to walk away then turned and nonchalantly asked, "Hey Larry did you cut yourself the other night?"

"What do you mean, Hal?"

"Well, I think it was Thursday you came in with blood on your shirt. You ran by the snack bar. Remember, we were sitting there?"

"No, I didn't cut myself. Barry smacked me in the nose at karate practice and I wiped the blood on my t-shirt. I had another one in my locker, so I just washed my face, changed my shirt and went to my work out. It wasn't a big deal. Why do you ask?"

"Curious, I just remembered it that's all. You guys enjoy your workout. I'd better get back to work, myself."

Hal played 30 minutes of racket ball with Bucky before the second session with Mrs. Thompson. By the time he got to the snack bar the others were about ready to call the police on their own, which was unheard of. To make a decision without Hal was almost a mutiny in his eyes.

"Larry has a perfectly good explanation for what happened with his t-shirt. He said that his friend Barry hit him in the face in karate practice."

"Then why is he hiding the evidence?"

"He wasn't hiding it, Kesha. He just missed the trash can when he was trying to throw it away."

"Well, I'm more worried about Jarrod now, anyway. Bertha said she can't tell him to call you cause he ain't answering her either. This ain't like Jarrod. Now we got two missing persons to worry about."

Hal stopped sipping his coffee and thought hard about what Mrs. Stallings had said about her daughter, 'it wasn't like her to do this' and now Kesha said the same thing about Jarrod. And even more obvious, yet Hal hadn't thought of it, Jarrod had the same letters as Barry and Larry. It could be a coincidence, but he didn't think so. Now we got two missing persons to worry about…"Oh, Hell," Hal shouted.

The others stopped talking to stare at him.

"It isn't Barry or Larry, it's Jarrod that she ran off with."

"That who ran off with?" Molly asked.

"Leslie Ann Stallings," Hal answered.

"No," Lakesha shook her head, "she's dead, Larry murdered her."

"They left together that night when she met him here. Remember, we couldn't figure out why Jarrod was coming back to work after his shift was over? He was meeting Leslie. Then, the next night they decided to go somewhere together."

"That's just a lot of speculation, Hal," Molly waivered a bit.

"Well, it makes more sense than believing that Larry murdered her."

Lakesha shook her head, "It just don't sound like something that Jarrod would do. I been knowing him all his life. He's a good boy."

"This doesn't make him a bad boy. It's just two young people starting a relationship. They do strange things," Hal countered.

"I agree with Hal," Billy said. "Jarrod told me he was happy now with his new girlfriend."

They all turned on Billy. "Why haven't you told us that before," Manny shouted.

"We weren't talking about Jarrod and a girl. Now we are," he was on the verge of tears.

Molly put her hands on Billy's arm, "Calm down Billy. Did Jarrod say who the girl was?"

"No! He just said that she was not like other girls he knew. She was serious about her education, and she was smart."

Lakesha stood and put her arms around the distraught desk clerk, "That sounds like Jarrod. He's a smart boy and likes girls that didn't act all silly. Thanks for remembering, Billy."

"I don't know, Hal. I guess it makes sense, but we still don't know where Jarrod and Leslie are," Manny said. "I guess we better start thinking about that."

"Right now, I think we all better go back to work. We'll talk about it later."

Hal was on cruise control. His mind wasn't on his job but on the events of the past few days. He felt that he was right about Leslie and Jarrod meeting at Castle of the Gods, but he also believed that they wouldn't just leave without letting their mothers know where they were. They were unable to contact them for some reason. He resolved to call the police and let them know what he knew. They could check hospitals to see if they were injured somehow. Some detail kept nagging at the back of his mind. Something that had a bearing on the case. But he couldn't quite put his finger on it. He decided to see if Manny could help.

'I can't think of anything new, Hal. We've been over it and over it. It all comes back to Larry and his bloody shirt. I just don't believe his story. He looked too worried when he ran by us that night. His shirt was way bloodier than just from a nosebleed. Plus, he was soaking wet."

Hal sat up straighter as he thought back, "That's right, it was raining hard that night. Everyone who came in was soaked. And that was the night Leslie met Jarrod. It rained all night because it was raining that morning when we left work."

"Yeah, but so what? What's that got to do with anything?"

"Manny, you grew up here, where do the kids go when they want to be alone?"

"We would go to Branson's Lane over behind the Fair Grounds or if you really wanted to be alone, you'd go to Harvey Point up on the Bluffs. Good place to park and the view is fantastic. Wait, what are you thinking, Hal? No one would go there in the rain. That road is narrow and steep."

"Let's drive up there after work, Manny. How long does it take to get there?

"About 15 minutes from here."

The sun was just beginning to rise when they finally left in Manny's car to drive to the local area called the Bluffs. Hal didn't have much hope of finding anything, but he had to try. Doing nothing was not an option.

"If we don't find anything I say we stop at the police station on the way back," Manny suggested.

"I agree. We'll tell them everything we know, which isn't much but probably more than they know. We don't have any proof that Leslie even came to the Castle let alone met Jarrod there. It's all circumstantial but I think we should tell them."

They drove past the high school, then the Walmart, Home Depot and the various fast-food restaurants. The commercial buildings faded behind as they entered farming country for about four miles. They turned off onto a little used road that narrowed as they drove through a small meadow and up an incline into the trees.

"Wow, I see what you mean about no one coming here in the rain," Hal said as they drove through the trees gaining altitude at every bend in the narrow road. Manny accelerated up a steep slope that was covered in ruts.

"Wait, Manny, stop. Look at those ruts. Someone did come up here in the rain."

Hal jumped out of the car. They were about halfway up the slope. He ran back down the hill and followed the ruts to the edge of the road where it dropped off steeply into a gully about 60 feet below. It was obvious there had been a disturbance like some trees had fallen over in a mud slide. Then he saw it.

"Manny, come here quick. Hello, can you hear me," Hal shouted down the hill.

"What is it, Hal?" Manny searched the ravine.

"Look, can you see it. A wheel sticking out under that tree there at the bottom."

'Oh my God, I do see it. Listen! I thought I heard something."

They stood still but couldn't be sure they heard anything other than the wind rustling the trees and the highway noises in the distance.

"Manny, get on your cell phone. Call for help. I'm going down there."

"Hal, I don't think you should it's too steep."

"Just call 9-1-1, Manny." Hal studied the situation and thought if he went higher, he could use the contour of the grade and tree branches to traverse down and reach the car.

"Hal, no signal," Manny shouted. "I'm going to drive up to the point and see if there's a signal there. I can't turn around here anyway.

"Go. I'll be alright."

Hal began having second thoughts as he plunged off the edge of the road. The slope was gradual for the first ten feet then quickly dropped off until almost vertical. He slipped on the leaves and rocks grabbing tree limbs and roots, whatever he could to slow his descent. He took a serpentine route to the bottom and had to crawl over trees, some pulled violently from their shallow grip in the rocky soil. He could see the car from about twenty feet. It was on its roof. Trees had crashed down on it essentially covering the vehicle from the road.

"Can you hear me?" he shouted.

"Yes, help me, please," a girl's voice sobbed.

Hal froze at the word me. Was she the only one who had survived?

"Hang on, help is coming."

He was surprised that anyone survived. The roof was caved in. Obviously, they slid down the road backwards and over the edge with the car flipping onto its roof when it reached the steepest part of the gully, then sliding the rest of the way tearing at the rocks and trees as it fell. He climbed down and peered into the narrow slot where the passenger window had been.

"Are you Leslie," Hal asked calmly? Her face was badly bruised with a large gash on her forehead.

"Yes," She sobbed.

"Who else is in there?"

"Jarrod and he's hurt bad. We've been here for days."

"I know Leslie. I have help on the way." Hal glanced up the hill hopeful that Manny would be there. He began surveying the scene trying to imagine how to get them out. He couldn't do it alone. It was going to take special equipment, Jaws of Life, a wrecker, a winch, chain saws. He circled the car as best he could, talking as he went.

"I spoke to your mother, Leslie. She knew you wouldn't leave without a word. She really loves you." He couldn't reach the driver's side window because trees and rocks blocked that side.

Hal peered back in the passenger window, "Jarrod are you awake?" A weak yes gave Hal a great sense of relief.

"Is that you, Hal?"

"Yes, it is, Buddy. I've got help on the way."

"I thought I was dreaming and back at the Castle. How did you get here?"

"It's a long story. We talked to your mom; she's really worried about you. When both of you went missing, I just started thinking about what happened. It's just a lucky guess but Manny and I came out here looking for you."

"Manny's here too?"

"Yeah, we all worked it out together. Lakesha called your mom and I talked to Leslie's mom."

Hal continued talking just to keep them occupied. He was beginning to worry because it was starting to cloud up again and another rainstorm could start the car sliding further down the gully. Then he heard the sirens.

"Hal, they're coming," Manny shouted. "They made me stay on the phone with them until they got close."

Hal could hear the trucks grinding up the last hill and then down the incline to where Manny was parked. He could hear voices but couldn't make out what they were saying.

"Hal, are you down there?"

"Yes, is that you, Bill," Hal shouted recognizing the fire chief's voice. "Who all's up there?"

"Right now, just me and Randy Johnson but I have a everyone on the way. I need to make an assessment. What will we need down there?"

Hal told them of his quick survey. He watched as Randy rappelled down with the winch cable from the Chief's large SUV.

"Hey, Hal, fancy meeting you here," the affable young fireman said. "I haven't seen you in a while. I changed shifts; now I work out during the day."

"That's what I heard, Randy. Good for you," Hal realized that Randy was making a point of being calm for the sake of Leslie and Jarrod.

"What have we got here?" He bent down to the smashed window.

"Hello, Miss, tell me your name and your injuries."

"Is that you, Randy, Jarrod whispered?

"Jarrod?"

Hal suddenly sensed more people coming down the slope. He moved out of the way as the emergency response team rappelled down. He acknowledged them in turn as most of them worked out at the Castle.

"Damn, Hal, I never expected to see you here."

"It's a long story," Hal replied several times. He looked for a route to get out of the ravine because he was in the way with all the new firemen, EMT's and police.

"Here, Hal," Randy indicated a harness attached to the cable he had arrived on. Hal buckled into the body harness and was slowly winched back up the slope. Manny and Lakesha applauded as he came over the crest of the road.

"Knock it off you guys," he said laughing. They hugged and laughed some more.

"Are they ok?" Lakesha asked, "Bertha's on the way and Mrs. Stallings too. You saved em, Hal."

"No, we all did," he gave Lakesha a big hug. "But they're in pretty bad shape. Beat up and I think Jarrod has broken bones. What time is it? I'm exhausted and there isn't anything we can do here. I need to go home and get some sleep. I have a date with Barbara tonight."

"Not me," Manny said, "I'm stayin' till they get them out of there. I can't get out anyway until all the emergency vehicles leave."

"I ain't leaving either," Lakesha announced. "But you can take my car home. I'll ride with Manny or Bertha when she gets here. Just leave the keys in it."

"Where's your car?"

"Down at the bottom of the hill. They won't let anybody into the gate off the highway but it's that Wainwright boy guarding, and I told him he best get outta my way or I'd tell his wife he's been making eyes at Donetta Mays. He moved right quick. I told him to let Bertha and Mrs. Stallings in too. He's a terrible guard."

Hal took the keys and laughed all the way down the hill. Small towns, he thought. The drive home was uneventful, and he fell into a deep sleep with his alarm set for five that evening. The six hours of sleep left him groggy and disoriented. But he brightened when he thought of Barbara waiting for him.

"You've had a busy day," she greeted him with a beautiful smile, even teeth and a bronze glow on her skin that wasn't from a bottle or the sun, just natural. Hal couldn't believe his luck. He wanted to be cautious and move slowly but everything told him that she was the one for him.

"I never thought I would feel this way again."

"What way?" she asked.

"That you are a very special woman, and I can't wait to get to know you better."

"That's an interesting answer to my comment that you've had a busy day."

"How do you know?" he asked.

"Talked to Lakesha and Molly. They told me the whole story."

"You probably know more than me, then. How are they? I fell asleep as soon as I got home and haven't checked my messages."

"Jarrod is hurt pretty badly; I think broken ribs and his right arm. Both of them have concussions and Leslie has some deep cuts that will leave scars, but they'll survive."

"Great news! I'm glad all of that is over. I need to go back to being just a personal trainer and forget the detective business," he was disappointed that she ignored his feelings. They sat in silence waiting for their food.

Barbara smiled at him again, "What?" he grinned.

"That was difficult for you, wasn't it?"

"No, not really. At first, I was worried about getting down to the car, but it wasn't as steep as..."

"No, silly," she laughed, "I mean sharing how you feel. That was difficult. You're not used to it."

"Oh!" he nodded, "but it's not that. It's more that I haven't had these feelings in a long time. I'm kind of nervous I guess. I shouldn't feel this way at my advanced age."

"Well, if it makes you feel any better, I'm nervous too and I can't wait to get to know you better. I think we'll have a lot of fun in the process."

The next morning, when Hal finally reached home, he decided to read his messages. There were many including a picture sent by Lakesha. It showed Senator Vandergrift and his wife along with Larry and another girl identified as Larry's sister. The message from Lakesha was, 'Barbie ain't Ken's momma. We got to call the police.'

The message from Manny read, 'Jarrod didn't quit. Bif made that up. We've got to call the Big Guy.'

Hal texted them both, 'Just calm down. It will hold until Monday. There has to be a logical explanation.'

He fell asleep accompanied by the image of his new friend, her head back laughing at one of his silly jokes. Life appeared to be getting better by the minute. He didn't give one thought to the new mysteries at the Castle of the Gods.

THE BITTER FRUIT OF ANGER

There was a time when my life seemed complete. I was in love, and I knew what love meant...what it felt like. The years before the rancid seeds of jealousy grew into an anger I could not control. I basked in a glow of self-confidence knowing that I treated everyone equally; secure in the knowledge that as a man and with all good intentions, I could do no wrong. A time of ignorance, free from the constraints of honesty or caring about the effects of my actions. A time when I felt that life was perfect because I worked hard and provided well, and I was always there for my family.

I stood silently staring out to sea. The sun, slipping away, bathed my face in warmth but couldn't soothe the pain of the love I am sure I've lost forever. Orange-red sparks set the sparce clouds ablaze. Waves caressed the shore, endless and forever, sometimes furious like time dwindling away. A stiff breeze from the Sea of Cortes blew steady, one of the four strong winds that don't change...come what may. But we change, we mere humans and I could cry for the life I've wasted, but I won't because it wouldn't mean a thing. Yet, if I could, I would go back in time somehow, because I know just what I would change.

I stood silently thinking. I was so...what's the word I'm looking for? I was so wrapped up in myself, with what I was doing...I forgot Maria's birthday, but we kidded about it. I thought she was ok with it. Then I forgot Mother's Day. Just like what happened with Karen. God, I wish I could go back and start over again. Maybe I should go back to Texas. I don't think I can fix it this time...beg Maria to come back like I have so many times before.

I stood silently weeping.

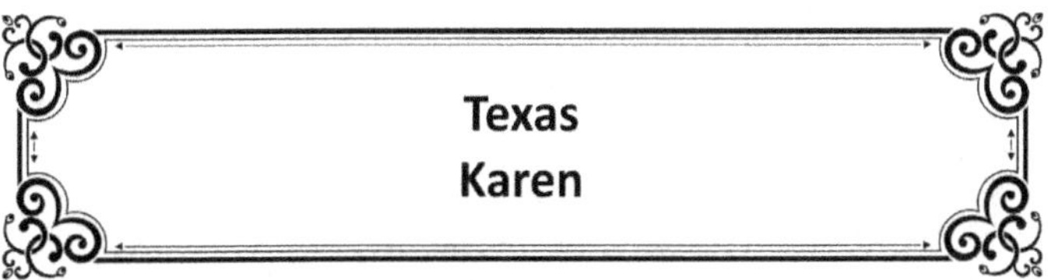

Crystal put her hand on my shoulder, "Daddy, are you ok? What are you looking at?"

I must have been staring into space, trying to digest the implications of the phone records spread on my desk. Karen called the number over 50 times this month at different times of the day and night. But whose number is it?

Crystal shook me a bit, her reddish blonde hair and blue eyes made me feel I was looking in a mirror. "Sorry Honey! I was daydreaming."

"Really, you think? Wake up Dad, Linda's mom wants to talk to you."

"Where is your mom?" I asked, but she and Linda were already dashing up the stairs.

"Hello Riley," Sheila glanced down at the phone invoice. I covered it with the newspaper, trying to control my anger; I had suspicions but nothing concrete until now. I know my cheeks are flushed. Could it be Bill, Sheila's husband? He's a good-looking guy definitely Karen's type. Sheila has put on quite a bit of weight in the past five years. Her hips are wider than her shoulders. "She let herself go to seed," Bill told me over drinks after the Longhorn game a couple of weeks ago.

I tried to be nonchalant, "How's Bill doing? I haven't seen him lately. More hours at Dell?"

She turned away, "I haven't seen him much either," then quickly added, "evidently he has to work late every evening." She glanced back at my desk, at the newspaper, "Where's Karen?"

"Probably ran to the store. It's going to be a long night," I tried to smile, "What did you want to ask me?"

"What time shall I pick Linda up in the morning?"

"Whenever you get around. I don't have anything to do but make breakfast for a bunch of fourth graders."

She turned to leave, "Don't worry, I can show myself out."

The chair almost fell over when I jumped up, "Oh, hell, I'm sorry Sheila."

She laughed, but in a good-natured way, "Oh come on, Riley, I was just kidding. Stay here, I can see you're busy with something important." She gestured at the phone invoice peeking from under the paper like a church lie on Sunday.

When I looked back, she was gone. Through the window I could see others arriving. Some carrying presents for Crystal. Sheila stopped to talk with Hector Torrez. His son, Raul, climbed out of the back seat of the truck with a small present. Raul had a crush on Crystal and Hector was a good friend. We joined his family, wife Loretta, and two kids, in San Antonio for a long weekend last month and enjoyed it tremendously. Good people! I might confide in him. No, I better keep everything to myself. Probably nothing to it. I'll just start paying more attention to Karen. I've been so busy managing the house, the kids, and my properties.

It seems like we just brought Crystal home from the hospital. A complete surprise, I didn't care if I had any more kids at 40. I had three from my first marriage, but it was a joy from the time I first set eyes on her. Then we planned for Henry but only because everyone assumed I wanted a boy. I truly didn't care but I love him to pieces. He's a handful though. In fact, I'd better find out where he is. He'll be tormenting Crystal's friends.

He was in his room sitting quietly hidden in his fort, the cardboard box the refrigerator was packed in, "What's up son? You sad about something?"

"Crystal yelled at me."

She is six years older and a bit jealous of him since she was the princess until he came along and took her crown, at least in her mind. We love them both, and my three daughters from the marriage to Cheryl. They are with us most of the time now. Lots of reasons why but mainly because Cheryl just doesn't have time for them. It's hard on Karen because she has her own career, and she is 12 years younger than me. I don't think that's our problem though, but it contributes. Mainly, I just don't have a lot of time to do the things she enjoys doing like go out to honky-tonks drinking and dancing every weekend. Someone has to watch the kids and I trust her, or I did until I saw the phone records. My God, I hope there's a good explanation. I love her so much it takes my breath away even after twelve years together.

"Why did your sister yell at you?"

"Just because I wanted to play catch with Raul like we did in San Antonio."

"Come on, let's go downstairs. Climb on my back; I'll play catch with you while Crystal and her friends have the birthday party."

I bounced him up and down walking down the stairs, turned the corner and there standing behind the open door where no one from the outside could see them was Hector Torrez with his hands wrapped around my wife, fondling her ass. Karen spied me immediately, pulled away, and reached for her eye, "Oh thanks, Hector, you got it."

She looked at me, "I had something in my eye. He got it thought," and she darted into the kitchen. I was too startled to say anything. Henry was still kicking at my sides, urging me to bounce.

"I gotta run, Riley! See you in the morning when I come back for Raul. Take care." Hector practically ran to his truck. I tried to catch my breath, but that made it worse. I started sweating and sat down in the recliner letting Henry crawl into my lap. He sensed something was wrong and put his arms around my neck, but didn't say anything.

Karen hurried out of the kitchen and ruffled Henry's hair without looking at me, "You two need to start the grill and get the burgers and hotdogs going." She couldn't have been more composed or any cheerier.

I was fuming, I know what I saw, but what can I say now; why didn't I say something the moment I saw them? Crystal, Linda and Raul charged into the living room, "Daddy, everybody is starving, and Mom says I can't open any presents until after we eat. Come on," she grabbed my arm to pull me up. Henry joined her, getting behind me and pushing. I was so angry I couldn't think straight. My good friend, and my wife, help me Lord, it can't be true.

At eleven o'clock the kids were in the game room watching a movie, eating popcorn, and drinking sodas. Karen was cleaning the kitchen, pretty much ignoring me while I glowered at the phone records in my study. Angrier and angrier my temper was boiling. I know the warning signs, but I can't help myself. I know I'm going to regret this, but I grabbed the invoice and stormed into the kitchen, my face flushed and breathing heavily.

"What's going on? Are you having an affair with Hector?"

She looked up from the sink, shock or surprise spread across her face, I couldn't tell what it was.

"Are you crazy, Rilcy, what are you talking about?"

"Whose phone number is this?"

She glanced at the crumpled paper I held two inches from her face, "I don't know."

"You don't know?" I shouted, "It's your phone, how can you not know who you called 50 times this month?"

Henry charged into the room, "Daddy come on, Crystal's friend spilled his coke on the movie player."

With hands balled into fists, I glowered at her daring her to say something. Henry grabbed my arm pulling me toward the game room. I glanced back as we went through the door. She was reaching for her phone.

The kids didn't notice anything amiss, I am sure, but I was fuming mad the entire evening. Crystal and Linda held court over their domain deciding which games to play, which movies to watch and when to go swimming. I scowled at Karen every time she walked by even though she was the epitome of poise and charm. We finally got them calmed down at one in the morning, at least enough that they all found a spot in the game room, and some were asleep while others talked quietly, a few played Monopoly. I did everything I could think of to stay busy and keep my mind off the phone records and images of Karen and Hector that kept floating through my mind. At midnight I cleaned the grill, swept the patio, and vacuumed the pool. I didn't finish until 2:20. I still wasn't tired. Lightning was visible on the northwest horizon and occasionally a few rumbles of thunder. I hoped it wasn't a bad storm to keep the kids awake.

At 3 A.M. the phone records were spread out before me in the study, and I sat with my head in my hands. Karen was sound asleep or pretended to be when I went into the bedroom, so I moved into Henry's room and watched him innocently sleeping in the top bunk, then crawled into the bottom.

"Daddy, wake up!" Henry had a hand on each side of my face shaking me awake. I'm glad he's not any stronger, might have strained my neck. "Why are you in my bedroom, daddy?" He seemed a bit indignant about the situation.

"You were having a bad dream son. I just meant to lay down for a minute."

"But you have all your clothes on," he was very suspicious.

"I better go check on Crystal and her friends. You want to come with me?

"No, I have to go to the bathroom."

"You need my help?"

Quite crossly he scowled, "I'm not a baby."

No one was stirring in the game room, but it was only 6:30. I dreaded going into the bedroom, dreaded the inevitable confrontation, knowing that I wouldn't be able to control my temper. It is a terrible curse; I hate people who can be so calm when they have been wronged or think they have. I can't do it; my emotions are there for everyone to see. No one was in the kitchen, so I made coffee then sat on the back porch just staring into space.

The back door opened, I turned, thinking it was one of the kids. Karen was still in her pajamas carrying a cup of coffee. She leaned down and kissed my cheek, "Good morning, handsome. You were up late last night."

That certainly wasn't what I expected. She pulled the chair next to me with the cup on the patio table, "Beautiful morning, isn't it?"

Looking around I realized the heat had abated a bit with the thunderstorms last night, "Yes, it is, but I hadn't noticed. I've been thinking about all those phone calls you made to that unknown number you didn't recognize."

"You are a big ole mess, you jealous thing. That's Hector's new phone he uses for the fantasy football league," she took a sip of the coffee. "He asked you to be in it, but you said no. So, I tried it…It's fun."

"Are you serious, Karen? Why is this the first I've heard anything about it?"

"You weren't interested, I was."

The back door flew open. Linda stormed out, "Mr. D., Lamar is mooning everybody." Her Texas drawl in full force, "I for one, am not impressed with his skinny ass and I'd appreciate it if you would make him quit." Lord, she sounded just like her mom.

I figured I better get in there and resolve it before Sheila arrived and raised hell. Lamar was a little hellion and I wish Crystal wouldn't have invited him. I was convinced that Karen was lying. She wouldn't know fantasy football from real football. But what the hell am I going to do about it now?

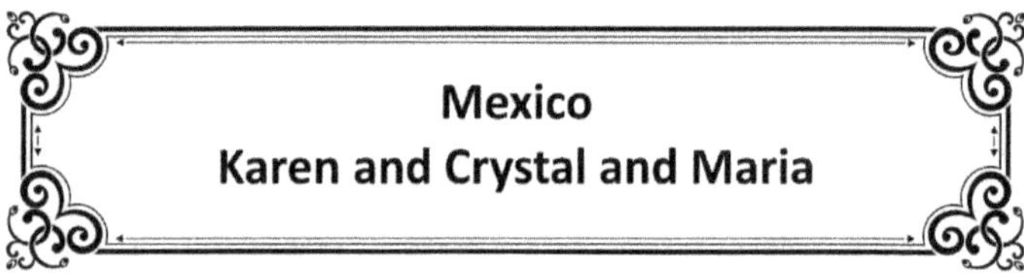

The sea was angry, and I could smell rain on the slight breeze. I don't think Karen or Crystal could tell any difference. We were just finishing our breakfast, fashionably late, the Mexican way. Attentive waiters cleared away the detritus from our leisurely meal. This restaurant is popular with tourists, the sounds of the ocean just a few feet away. It was not a place I would normally visit.

"Do you think it will go the other way, Dad?"

"What?" Karen glanced up from the Spanish newspaper that she couldn't read.

"The hurricane, Mom. We've been talking about it for ten minutes."

Karen looked at me for the answer. Her beautiful blue eyes framed by dark lashes and hair. A brief memory flashed, lingering from our wedding day or maybe the day we divorced, I suddenly couldn't remember. Both were long ago.

"We haven't had a bad one here in over 30 years. I don't think we have anything to worry about."

"I just hope it doesn't delay our flight."

"It wouldn't bother me. I'd stay a few days longer if I didn't have to go back to work. This has been just what I needed, Dad."

"You can stay longer in March, Crys and the weather won't be so hot."

"It's so nice of you to let mom come with me."

"Absolutely no problem. I'm glad you both could come," I lied. Karen invited herself and paid her own way. I suppose I could have said no.

I was sitting with my back to the entrance. Karen recoiled in surprise her brow furrowed. There was a commotion behind us. Our waiter paused, his hand resting on my coffee cup. He turned to face the threat whatever it was. Reflexively I swiveled, taking the slap on the side of my head. There was an angry force behind it. I started to rise…"Cabrón! Mentiroso! Nunca te volveré a ver," She threw the gold necklace at me, but I ducked. It hit Karen on the chin, the cross lodged in the neckline of her blouse, sparkling in the mid-morning light. The waiter 's eyes were fixed on the precarious nature of the expensive jewelry. I turned only to see Maria brush the startled patrons aside as she rushed from the restaurant. Crystal's eyes were wide when I turned back. Karen pulled the necklace from her blouse, "Well, I take it this was a gift she wanted to return," handing it across the table.

Crystal burst out laughing, "Awkward! But she is beautiful, Daddy."

"And young," Karen laughed the same false laugh I grew to detest years ago.

I wanted to rush after Maria, hold her, make her understand this is my family. Not a threat to her. I continued to watch the empty aisle hopeful she would return. Even her anger excites me. When I turned back, Karen and Crystal were watching me, "Sorry about that," was all I could mumble.

I texted a stanza from Ella Wheeler Wilcox to her WhatsApp
"I love your arms when the warm white flesh
Touches mine in a fond embrace;
I love your hair when the strands enmesh
Your kisses against my face."

But she didn't respond. I don't know how she knew we were at Pablo's. Maybe she's been following me. I asked for the check. I'm glad we were finished eating, I didn't want to discuss it any further.

Later, it got so hot we were forced to seek the shade of the old kiosk with its sagging roof bearing the weight of the forgotten dreams of the Revolution that it was built to celebrate. The beautiful twin towers of the Cathedral loomed over us, the tops just visible at the ridgeline of the drooping monument. Dark hair plastered to her forehead, Karen fanned furiously with the Spanish language newspaper, "My God how do people live here?" A rhetorical question both Crystal and I ignored.

The bells began to chime startling the pigeons who swept into the air like ocean spray only to settle back where they started. "Shoo," Karen futilely waved the newspaper then glanced at the steeple as the bells began to ring, "Ask not for who the bell tolls…"

"Mom, that's not how it goes," Crystal interrupted, "We've told you this before," She looked to me for support, "Dad, do you want to tell her, again."

"Never send to know for whom the bell tolls…it tolls for thee."

Karen looked the other way, fan still waving, "I say it like everyone else does. Why is that a crime with you two? You always do this to me." The fan became a blur.

"You're right! It's not a big deal." I put my hand on her shoulder. She pulled away.

An old man, draped in rags, carrying a plastic bag full of cans, stopped in front of Karen. She recoiled at his outstretched hand and incoherent babble. He was saying, in Spanish, that she was a beautiful woman and he hoped she could spare a few pesos for an old grandfather down on his luck.

"Oh my God, Riley, make him go away," she turned her shoulder to him. I gave him all the coins in my pocket, no more than fifty pesos, but he was satisfied and shuffled off.

She glared angrily at me, "Look at you," she sobbed. "Living in this terrible place with beggars everywhere and suddenly you're dressing like a rock star. I tried to get you to dress nice for years, but you didn't care and now you look like a fashion model, I guess for your Mexican whore."

"Now wait a minute, Karen, she's no more a…"

"Mom, stop it right now. You promised not to do this. Dad has lived here for 15 years; you have no right."

Karen started crying. I tried to comfort her, but I was still angry for calling Maria a whore. Crystal started for the church, "Come on you two. Let's go see how outlandish the Catholics have made this one. You can wallow in your guilt in there."

Karen dabbed at her eyes, "Stop being so dramatic Crystal Gale, if you could manage to keep a boyfriend for more than a week, you would understand."

Crys, stopped in the middle of the road, halting traffic, "Don't take your failures out on me, Mother. You're the one that cheated on Dad. It's not my fault you screwed up your life. If I was Dad, I wouldn't let you within a hundred miles of me."

I grabbed Karen by the arm, hustled her toward Crys, grabbed her arm and drug them both across the narrow street, "Ok, stop it, both of you. Don't ruin the trip on the last day. Let's finish our tour of the church and go find something cool to drink."

I was growing weary of their bickering. I wanted to find Maria and sit with her in the Cantina holding her hand. Her face taunted me from the shadows of last week before Crystal and her mom arrived. We had such a wonderful time, dinner at Edwardo's, walking on the beach, and waking up the next morning in each other's arms.

The church nave was cool like placing your cheek against a damp marble statue. There were many people inside as the faithful prepared for Dia de los Muertos. We hurried through, not wanting to bother anyone. A wedding party was forming, two of the wealthy families in town. I had a passing acquaintance with the patriarch of the bride and thought it best to offer my congratulations for the wedding of his granddaughter to another wealthy landowning family. It was advantageous for both. I couldn't help but wonder how willing the bride and groom were, but they looked happy. The bride wore her white gown demurely. The bridal party carried on with pictures visiting among themselves while the poor shuffled around them to ply their faith in the coolness of the marble statues weeping and stained-glass casting rays of light onto the nave.

Stepping from the church, the sun was like a heat lamp bathing our faces and burning our eyes as we scrambled for the dark glasses. There was still a bit of shade on the west side of the street, so we single filed down the sidewalk to Patron's, a Mexican bar I know. They speak only Spanish so we would be free to visit uninterrupted and the beer was very cold. Karen drank wine.

"What did you think of the Cathedral?"

"You know what I think about Catholics, Riley," Karen put her dark glasses on the table and glared at me. She was raised Southern Baptist.

"They make a pretty cool church. Those stained-glass windows must have cost a fortune. And I think some of that gold plate was real on the Throne of God, or whatever it was," Crystal took a big drink from the bottle of Pacifico. "Wow! That is cold. I love this place."

"It all disgusts me. Those poor people without money for food. Yet they give to the church. What hypocrites."

"Mom, it is called faith and they take great pride in it."

"I have faith in the one true God, and we don't need Jesus hanging on the cross with blood dripping off his body."

"What do you guys want to do this afternoon?" They both stared at me.

Crystal took another pull on the beer, "You want to hike up to the lighthouse?"

"Oh my God, no. It's too hot," Karen sipped her wine. "How old is that girl, Riley?"

"What girl?" I looked around the bar.

"Don't play stupid. Your girlfriend or whatever she is."

"Mom, you make girlfriend sound dirty."

Karen shrugged and raised her wine glass for a refill.

I tried to think of something to say, and opted for the truth. "She's older than she looks, 55, if that's really important."

Crystal was truly surprised, "Wow! I would have guessed in her early 40's."

"She's a wonderful person, but she has a temper."

Karen laughed, her sincere laugh, "Well, ya think?" She drained her glass, "Order me another. I'm going to pee."

"Don't go in here," I gestured to the door, "go outside and around the corner to your right. Casa de Piedra has excellent bathrooms. I don't want to hear you complain about the ones in here."

Crystal and I watched her leave.

"Sorry, Dad, she's turning into a bitter woman."

I shook my head and took a long drink from my beer. I ordered a Shrimp Diablo appetizer to snack, "Crys, I'm afraid time is passing me by."

"I've never heard you talk that way, daddy. What's wrong, are you sick again?"

I twirled my beer bottle watching the condensation flow down to the old wooden tables scarred from years of abuse, "No, just old, I guess."

"Is it the Mexican lady?"

I looked at her for a long time trying to answer that question for myself, forget about someone else, especially my daughter.

"Do you think she is just after your money?"

I had to smile at that, "Pretty much the standard line of thought, isn't it?"

She shrugged.

"That is something you would have to ask her."

"How can I? You didn't introduce us.

"I would have Crys, I wanted to, but your mom kind of complicated matters."

She nodded her head and hugged me, "Yes, I guess she did. But the trip hasn't been that bad, has it?

I shook my head no as Karen sat back down, "We should have gone to the bar over there. What a nice place."

Our phones began blaring with weather warnings. Advisories predicting hurricane landfall fifty miles either side of us.

"We're right in the middle," Crys held her phone for Karen to see.

Maria hurried past the front door going toward her mother's house on Calle Benito Juarez. I jumped up mumbling something about needing to check on my dog and ran after her grabbing her arm from behind, "Maria, please stop this. Why are you being so rude? It's only my daughter and her mother."

Her eyes burned with anger as she turned to face me, "I know who they are. Why is that woman in your bed?"

"Como? What are you talking about?"

"Irene told me her clothes are in your room, her nightgown is on your bed," she began crying silently, tears flowing down her cheeks, "You told me you didn't love her anymore, she meant nothing to you." She pulled away walking back toward Patron's wiping her eyes.

"Wait, Maria. Who told you that?"

"Irene."

"The maid?"

"She saw that woman's clothes in your bedroom."

I began to smile, "Listen to me my love, my daughter, and her mother sleep in my room on the big bed and I sleep in the guest room. They wouldn't be comfortable on that small bed."

Anger morphed into a smile that melted my heart. She threw her arms around my neck for a hug that lasted until I took her by the hand to meet my family.

My left knee rested in the dirt and with my right hand on the bumper I attempted to push myself up. After painfully restoring my legs, I leaned against the fender to catch my breath. I didn't find any lose wires under there, but I'm no mechanic. It must be the starter motor or some component.

A red rooster strutted by, glancing at me from time to time, its head bobbing to a primitive beat. I used my handkerchief to wipe my face and hands startling the rooster who stared at me suspiciously. The dusty parking lot contained a few nice cars from the hotel guests but also a collection of rusted and derelict automobiles from a bygone era. The rooster seemed to be the King of this domain.

Lenny, my mechanic in Mazatlán, warned me, "I wouldn't chance going out of town. That radiator leak isn't going to get smaller. It's not an emergency but we have to repair it. I just can't get to it right now. It's Semana Santa, Riley, stay here and enjoy the parade."

It was a long trip over the mountains on a snaky two-lane road with big speed bumps in every pueblo along the way. We were tired and sweaty, but a nice swim in the pool revived us. I came to get the car to drive into the village for dinner when I discovered it wouldn't start. The first thing I thought was battery, but that wasn't it. The lights all work. Why in the world didn't I listen to Lenny. But then, I chuckled to myself, it's not the radiator, not that it makes me feel any better.

Stretching my aching back, I brushed the dirt off my knees and started the painful walk back to the hotel. In Spanish, a voice called out, "Car trouble, senor?"

"Si, creo que es el motor de arrangue, my starter motor."

We continued, me in my halting Spanish and him excited to practice his few words of English.

"It is Semana Santa Senor, Pascua begins today. Nobody is working."

"That's what I've been told," I watched him, a slender man in the hotel uniform but not the neat clean garb of the maids and cooks. He was the handy man.

"Do you know of a mechanic who might come help me?"

"Yes, I know of two here in town, one is my cousin, but both are excellent."

I waited a moment to see if he would volunteer to call one for me. He simply repeated, "It is the beginning of Pascua they have already begun the celebrations. But Señora Lizaragua may know of someone." He referred to the manager of the hotel; a statuesque woman who seemed aloof and distant to me, but also very efficient.

"Maybe you could call your cousin and see if he will come look at the car."

He thought for a moment, then laughed, "He would say he will come but I know Jose very well and he is already drinking the tequila and cerveza. Even if he did come, I don't think he would do a very good job. It is best that you speak to Señora Lizaragua.

I hobbled back to the hotel to give Maria the bad news. She laughed in her good-natured way and put her arm around my waist as we walked to the lobby, "Well you were worried for car trouble it is just different trouble than you expected."

The hotel is very old, but well preserved with thick walls and lush vegetation in the courtyard and large planters in the common areas. We found Señora Lizaragua at the reception desk, a tall woman, almost as tall as my six feet. She listened sympathetically while I explained, then said, "It is Semana Santa and Pascua."

I nodded my head as though it was the first time I heard of this.

"No one will be working," she continued, thinking I didn't understand.

I took a deep breath to show I was thinking profoundly of this troubling situation while internally, I was growing frustrated, "But you do know of mechanics in town that could help under normal circumstances, correct?"

"Oh yes, there are two excellent mechanics in town. One is my nephew, but I know they will not want to work on the holiday. Maybe Monday if they aren't busy or still recovering from the weekend."

Well, this is wonderful, everyone in town is related and they all know each other well enough that they can read minds. I tried the direct approach, "Maybe you could try to call them anyway. What are we to do, we need to be back in Mazatlán on Monday for work. But it is what it is. If that is the case and we have to stay Sunday night will our room still be available?"

"No, we are booked but I will find you a place to stay. My cousin has a room that she rents occasionally."

My back ached, I worried about what it would cost to get the car repaired and Maria's cheerful disposition didn't help. I felt she should be more concerned since she also had to work on Monday. We had no plans for Sunday because we expected to drive back home. Now with no transportation and everyone busy we would be stuck at the hotel all day, which on reflection didn't sound too bad. I could write and Maria could read and lie by the pool. Maria wasn't excited about packing up and moving to Señora Lizarraga's cousin's house and neither was I. It took forever to fall asleep Saturday night. Maria read love poems to me in Spanish. I didn't understand most of them, but she translated, and it was beautiful coming from her. The two lines I do remember from the last poem were: 'No dejo de extrañarte, Y no puedo dejar de amarte.' "I keep on missing you and I can't stop loving you" We finally fell asleep around two.

At 6:30 that morning Maria began shaking me gently awake. I wasn't sure where I was, "Someone is at the door," she pushed me to get up. I staggard over in my pajamas to find Señora Lizaragua smiling warmly, "The mechanic will be here at seven. You must meet him at your car with the key."

"You mean this morning," I tried to shake the cobwebs from my brain.

She glanced haughtily, "Of course I mean this morning. If it was in the evening, I wouldn't wake you now."

Maria laughed, "I heard what she said. He won't be here until 8 if he comes at all. Go back to sleep."

I laid down, closed my eyes, and tried to drift off, but sleep wouldn't come. I pictured the mechanic driving up in his big tow truck with cases full of tools and a winch to load the car if he couldn't fix it in the parking lot. For some reason I imagined it as big and red with Lizaragua Towing stenciled on the door panel. I kissed Maria on the cheek, got up, stretched my aching back, grabbed a cup of coffee from the restaurant to sit in the car and wait. I opened the hood then looked around for the rooster who was nowhere in sight. Seven came and went, Seven-thirty then eight. Maybe I could have slept if I wouldn't have had the coffee. I leaned back in the seat and thought wearily of where I was. A dusty little town in the Sierra Madres with a broken-down car at the mercy of strangers, all related, who spoke a different language and celebrated Easter drinking tequila.

Getting out of the car I heard the noise of an old motorbike pulling into the driveway. It pulled up behind the car bearing a middle-aged man in t-shirt, jeans, and flip-flops. On the back was a young boy of seven or eight, wearing an LA Dodgers baseball cap and carrying a small plastic container, black with a green lid. They both smiled pleasantly.

"Buenos Dias," he said, shutting down the motor. Without any pleasantries, he climbed off, took the plastic box from the boy and sat it on the fender, "Go ahead and try to start it," he said in his rapid colloquial Spanish. Taken aback at the abrupt turn of events, I didn't respond because I didn't understand a word he said.

He smiled at me again, as did the boy, and in halting English said, "start," pantomiming turning the key. I climbed achingly back into the car and turned the key over. Nothing!

He waved his hands to stop, opened the plastic box and pulled out some electric wires that appeared to be wrapped in insulation from the 1940's. Still sitting in the car, I couldn't see exactly what he was doing under the hood but in a few seconds the boy began pantomiming and said, "Start."

Again, nothing!

He reached back into the plastic box to retrieve another set of wires with what appeared to be knitting needles attached to a black box with a gauge of some kind. He began a running commentary, most of which I didn't understand except for occasional words, and he would throw in an English translation which I understood less than his Spanish. The words I understood were battery, starter motor, wires, springs, and solenoid. But I couldn't tell which was the problem or if he knew yet.

I didn't know his name or if he was related to the manager or the handyman, or both. I guess it doesn't matter but I think about things like that. I could see the dollar signs rolling over as the cash register was ringing up the butcher's bill, maybe as much as $10,000 or $15,000 pesos, $500 to $750 US dollars.

That is what I would pay in the US, or more. I was at his mercy. He sure seems like a nice guy. And the little boy was a delight, helping dad, communicating with me, and maintaining a cheerful attitude when he should have been home with his brothers and sisters celebrating the holiday.

Back to the plastic box he produced another device which he attached to the knitting needles then began poking and prodding in various hard to reach places. We practiced starting several more times when suddenly, the motor turned over and started right up. He hurried to the door, "Don't turn it off. Follow me to my shop. I can't fix it here...I need my tools."

He and the boy carrying the plastic box got back on the bike, pulled to the entrance, and waited for me. I had serious doubts that I would find the shiny repair shop with red cases full of tools and auto supplies from my daydreams. When we arrived, he gestured for me to wait and not turn off the car. I couldn't see through the wood fence surrounding his house, but he soon pulled an old rusty pickup into the street then a newer car to make room for me. I pulled into the driveway where there was a dusty yard with a comfortable house on the right and a shed of wood and corrugated tin dominating the premises. In some previous time, he or his father, or maybe his grandfather had dug a hole in the dirt and reinforced it with concrete. I pulled my car carefully over the hole and got out. The shop was disorganized with old tools, grease, auto parts, an old motorcycle with the engine lying next to it. He scurried about seeming to know where everything was, soon producing a powerful light which he shined into the engine, crawled into the hole, shined the light from below, then stood solemnly next to me. The starter motor was the problem, and he might be able to rebuild it in certain cases or replace the gears or springs in other cases, or if it wasn't repairable, he would have to order a new one and it would take a few days to arrive from Culiacan. It was all an uncertainty that he would not be able to resolve until he removed the starter motor. It would take at least three hours. I should go back to the hotel and wait.

The walk back took about 15 minutes through the town square. Maria was waiting, hungry, so we went straight to the restaurant. I explained what was happening, "See", she said, "you were all worried for nothing."

"Well, I'm still worried. I don't have much money and there is no ATM machine here."

"Riley," she looked at me with a smile that was full of love. I felt like the luckiest man in the world as she put her arm through mine and squeezed me close, "the mechanic will take care of it and we will find a way to pay him." Her beautiful smile reassured me more than her words. I scolded myself for being so nervous and took her in my arms for a warm embrace that lasted a long time, "I love you Maria and I know that I shouldn't worry so much, but I come from a long line of worriers. My mom used to come into our bedroom at night to make sure we were still breathing."

She laughed, "Well mothers are the same everywhere. I'm sure he is an honorable man and will do what he says. Try to relax and enjoy the meal. Why worry now?"

Later, I tried reading by the pool, but it was no use. I kept thinking of all the outcomes and none seemed positive. Maria fell asleep, untroubled. It was already two o'clock in the afternoon. Since I've known Maria, I try to be more positive about things but it's difficult for a natural born pessimist.

Suddenly, the handyman appeared smiling, "Your car is ready, Senor. It is parked in the front of the hotel. Arturo is waiting for you to pay him, and I will take him back to his house.

Startled, I didn't react for a moment. He began his explanation again, "No, I understood you, but I have to go get my wallet from upstairs. I followed him to the entrance where the mechanic, Arturo, waited, "I was able to rebuild the motor. You will be fine now, but there is a leak in the radiator you should have it fixed."

I was so surprised, it took me a few moments to respond, "Thank you very much! How much do I owe you?"

"I'm sorry for the high expense but it took a little longer than I thought. One thousand eight hundred pesos will cover everything," he handed me the key.

A little under $100 US dollars. I peeled off the money and added $200 pesos, "The extra is for bringing the car back to me."

He smiled as he put the money in his pocket, "Have that radiator checked when you get back to Mazatlán."

I waved as he rode away on the back of the handyman's motorbike and started back into the hotel to pack up for the trip back to Mazatlán. A nagging thought popped into my mind about midway through the lobby and I turned around to start the car. It fired right up, faster than ever. What was I worried about?

On the drive home, Maria reminded me that she was going on a motorcycle ride to Concordia with her friend Keith. I didn't think anything about it. She enjoyed riding on the back, and I didn't see any harm. I know he is a safe driver.

Mexico
Maria

It has been a year since our trip last Easter, just Maria and me. This year, the beach was crowded as far as we could see; cars lined the road on both sides with no place to turn around. I stopped at the resort to ask about a room, but I already knew the answer. The manager laughed at me, "It is Easter weekend, Senor, Semana Santa! No rooms, not here, not in Mazatlán or La Cruz," he shrugged the dismissive way that Mexican's say, 'it's out of my hands'.

Maria glared at me from the car. I sensed the tension during the drive, but I wasn't sure why. I was hot, frustrated, in no mood, "Why are you being so rude, Maria. We agreed to come without reservations. It's not just my fault."

"You insisted, I just consented because you never listen to me anyway. I knew this would happen." she texted furiously glancing at me with disgust.

"Who are you talking to? You've been on that phone since we left Mazatlán. Who are you talking to? "

"Social media. Facebook," she looked out the window but put the phone down.

I took a deep breath, watched her, growing more frustrated by the second. Something is up, but what? 'Don't accuse her of anything, Riley.' I thought to myself, 'it will just cause trouble.'

She began again with the texting. ''What are you doing?" I was growing frustrated again.

"Looking for a hotel room. Why don't you get your phone and try to help," she glared at me.

I pulled my phone from my pocket to see if I could find anything, but I knew it was useless.

"We could go to Cosalá," she held her phone to show me rooms available.

I dreaded that trip. Cosalá isn't far but the road is dangerous, winding through the mountains with topes lurking in every little Pueblo. Plus, I was worried about the car, old and beat up. My God, I'd hate to get stuck in the middle of the mountains on Easter weekend. There wouldn't be any help anywhere, but plenty of danger. I was lucky to find a mechanic last year and there are reports of Cartel activity here.

I glanced in the back seat where Maria's little girl was asleep, expecting to wake up at the beach.

"They have two pools," Maria seemed to anticipate my thoughts.

The trip was uneventful, although the sun was setting and on some of the curves it blinded me. In one tiny pueblo I failed to see a speed bump. We weren't going more than 20 but the impact was brutal, sending Kendra to the floorboard in the back seat. "Que Paso," she sobbed climbing back into the seat. I stopped along the road to be sure Kendra was not hurt and check the car as best I could. I didn't see any damage but, who knows. We drove into Cosala and found the hotel without problem.

After checking in, I parked the car in the adjoining parking lot. The two pools looked inviting after the tension filled drive, but first we decided to walk to a nice little restaurant we know in town. Right away it started when Maria stopped every twenty feet to take a picture of Kendra on the colorful streets and under the hanging decorations of umbrellas and flags. "Let's go eat and take pictures later. I'm afraid they'll close before we get there.

"Go on and eat if you are so impatient," she snapped.

"Whoa, Maria, what's going on? Why are you yelling at me?"

"I told you I wanted to show Kendra the town. If you don't want to join us, go on to the restaurant. I'm tired of telling you everything twice, sometimes three times. Try to pay attention instead of thinking of yourself all the time."

"I didn't know you meant right now. I thought you meant after we eat."

"You only hear what you want to hear. You disregard everything else then pretend like it didn't happen. Quit bullshitting me. You're just a typical jealous man trying to control me like I'm your property."

She was screaming at me by the time it ended. Kendra looked as shocked as I felt. Many tourists were in town for the Easter weekend. Those around us stopped to stare. I can only imagine what they thought, a beautiful young Mexican girl and her daughter with an old tall, graybeard gringo. I walked around them and went to the restaurant without a word to her.

The brightly lit, narrow streets with crowded ancient stone and brick buildings seemed to be choking the breath from my lungs. I know something is going on with her. She's been running around with younger motorcycle guys. I knew they were friends, but I didn't think it was anything more than that. Now I'm not so sure. I've got to compose myself before she gets here but I'm not going to apologize, she was rude to me, I didn't do anything. The waitress brought a bowl of chips, a bowl of salsa and a cerveza. My mind was wondering in a million directions generating scenarios that fit the narrative I was creating. She's become intimate with one of them, I know it. Wait, am I screwing up again, I feel it coming on. Fictitious scenarios are seldom right. Give her a chance to explain, Riley don't just blurt out accusations like you've done before...you idiot!

Sometimes I just feel lost. Here I sit, alone, in a forgotten, sleepy little Mexican village in the Sierra Madres waiting on a beautiful, angry, Mexican woman and her daughter. Tables full of families enjoying the cool of the evening surrounded me with a cat asleep on the window ledge and an old dog roaming around looking for a quiet corner to lay down. How the hell did I end up here so far from Texas and the life I used to know. I barely have enough Spanish to order the cerveza. Without Maria, I'm lost. What is going on? We've been good friends for ten years and lovers for four. I know I've screwed up time after time; just as we start growing close, I push her away...tell her to find someone her own age to hang with. Then the next week or the next hour I'm begging her to forget what I said and how I said it.

The old dog wandered over to look at me, commiserating or maybe just looking for companionship. "I feel your pain old boy," I rubbed his ears.

Maria and Kendra wondered in about then, "Perro, mama! Un perro Riley," she began hugging the confused but enthusiastic dog, wagging his tail as Kendra scratched his head.

"Are you finished being an asshole," Maria glared at me.

"Well, that comment doesn't help the situation. I didn't think I was being an asshole; I just asked a simple question." She sat down without comment and began again with the texting. I know she's talking to her new friend. I can tell just by the look of contentment on her face and right in front of me. This is really starting to make me mad. I try to compose myself for Kendra's sake.

"Look Riley, do you think he really likes me?" she said in her rapid child Spanish that I have a hard time following. I didn't answer because I didn't understand immediately what she said. I just smiled and patted both on the head.

"Why are you ignoring her? Answer her question," Maria glowered at me from across the table.

"Look, maybe you'll be happier having dinner without me," I stood up with both hands on the table towering over her.

"Sit down. Quit threatening me."

"I'm not threatening you, what is going on, Maria, why are you treating me this way?"

"Because you are acting like an immature child. I'm just re-acting to the way you are treating me."

I turned my attention to Kendra and the dog. I knew it would be fruitless to continue the discussion. Maybe we can calm down and discuss it tonight in the room. We didn't speak to each other the rest of the meal.

Later that night, we swam until the pool closed at 11, I took a shower and crawled into my bed while Maria and Kendra showered and put on their matching pajamas. Kendra crawled into bed with me for our pre-sleep ritual of translating words. I would point at something, and she would try to recall the English name then she would point at something, and I would try to name it in Spanish. She always beat me, but I didn't mind. She crawled into the other bed and immediately fell asleep. Maria sat on the edge of my bed, "What is wrong with you, Riley? Why are you acting this way?"

"I was going to ask you the same thing. It seems you spend more time talking to your friends in Mazatlán and on social media than you do with me and Kendra, or at least me."

She shook her head sadly, "We've had this conversation at least ten times. Yes, I have other friends, but you agreed that you wouldn't be jealous of them and yes, I ride on motorcycles with them, but it is just friendship. Why do you have to make everything about sex. It isn't like that; we are just friends."

"I'm not making it a sexual thing, Maria, it's about the commitment of time. I just feel that when you are with me you should focus on me and Kendra and when we get back home, and you are with them then focus on them."

"Riley, you are doing it again. You are letting your jealousy create imaginary things that aren't happening. You know I love to do Facebook and social media. All my friends do it. Just because you don't isn't a reason that I shouldn't."

I couldn't think of anything to say for the longest time. Finally, I blurted out, even though I knew I would regret it later, "So, are you having an affair with Keith?"

Her entire body sagged as she crawled into the bed with Kendra, "Oh my God, Riley, what is the matter with you? He is 21, he has a beautiful girlfriend. We are just friends, and I am tired of telling you this over and over. I can't deal with this anymore. Stop talking to me and go to sleep."

But I couldn't sleep and the next day when we arrived home, Kendra hugged me and said goodbye. Maria didn't even look at me.

UNDERTOAD

This morning, I made a cup of coffee and read the paper. Nothing unusual there. I've been reading the paper and having a cup of coffee every morning for 65 years. In my youth, I would sit with mother and sip her coffee while she read the paper. We read two newspapers then, one in the morning and one in the evening, the Rocky Mountain News and the Denver Post. I delivered them for years. I read the paper online now.

Why am I reflecting on these matters? I'll tell you why... because I am about to die.

It doesn't seem right that I die today. I'm a Cancer survivor, to die now after surviving lymphoma isn't fair. Hell, I know things, I met Ken Kesey for God's sake. I'm one of the few people in the world who has read and even partially understood Finnegan's Wake; not a particularly significant talent, but not one to be wasted. It would be a shame to die with no one even aware of my special gifts. I mention this because part of James Joyce's plot and imagery is about rivers, and I am in a river of shit right now. It's the California portion of the North Equatorial current, I think. A

*river in the ocean. How do I justify this Joycean reference? Because
I have discovered that my mind tends to wander when faced with
impending death.*

I've always been considered a little odd, growing up in a small,
ultra-conservative community where conformity was a virtue;
sports, hunting, drinking beer and rebuilding engines was the
norm. I was perceived as peculiar, a hazy-minded daydreamer
who spent hours reading.

In retrospect I never should have gone into the water, there
was no one else swimming and very few people even on the
beach. I took my wallet from my pocket, placed it in my shoe
and told Larry and Diane I was going to cool off. It felt like
100 degrees in the shade. We had just returned to Mazatlán after
walking up and down the sizzling streets of El Quelite; visiting
shops, eating at El Meson de los Laureanos, simply observing
the small town and its colorful inhabitants. A dip in the ocean
seemed logical.

I may have been giddy early on before the realization that I
was going to die. Panic occurs in that moment between experi-
encing life normally and the rude recognition that the irrevoca-
ble purchase of death has been receipted. Not a quick death in
this case, but one where there's time to draw buried memories
to the surface of consciousness, slowly developing a suggestion
of imminent disaster and then fully incorporating the reality.

I began to sense something was wrong, still, the feeling of
terror didn't occur immediately. There was a period of analysis,
of dawning, like a curtain going up to expectations of a kinder-
garten play but the scene onstage is from the Marquis De Sade.
Not giggly nervous children but grotesque creatures with faces
contorted in agony, their bodies twisted into demonic shapes.

I first rejected the concept like a business proposal to a conservative committee...nope, not interested, not gonna' happen. But then, the ugly truth takes time to congeal, like pudding in a mold.

It was a hot humid day, and I wasn't paying attention to the current. The waves were rough but mainly a nuisance. Mostly I was remembering the beautiful lady that I'd met in El Quelite. *What was her name? Maria something, refined yet funny and she spoke English well, much better than my Spanish, maybe I can see her again. She said that she lives and works in Mazatlán during the Tourist season. Maybe I'll go by her curio shop; I know where it is.*

But I can't, not yet, because I need to resolve this issue. Be positive, don't think of it as a problem. I'm not in a predicament; I have an opportunity to succeed, regardless of how bleak it looks. Swim hard for shore, I'm not that far out, swim hard, harder, but it's useless. What in the world is wrong with me? I'm a good swimmer, why can't I get out of this current?

Suddenly I panic. Bile heaves into my throat and I flail like an angry child denied a sugar candy; thrashing and churning like a wild man in an outnumbered fight, only my beating is administered by the lashing of the waves and the realization that I am going to die. A wretched sinking feeling of agony and fear grips me. Then a heavy wave washes over tumbling in a spin cycle. I can't tell the beach from the sea, my ass from my ankle. I gasp for air, gagging, and saltwater pours from my nose. This is complete terror... my God... the horror, I really am going to drown; please tell me it isn't happening. Try to touch the bottom, No! Keep your head up. Surely someone on the beach can see me, someone can hear me. But there is no one. I'm alone!

Stay calm, tread water... panic is what leads to death. The waves wash over me, filling my mouth and nose, this is unbearable. I feel like screaming. This is all so unnecessary, I shouldn't be drowning, I just wanted to cool off. Surely there must be someone on shore; I wave and yell, "Help me, help, please" but there isn't anyone and my voice drowns in the pounding surf lashing the shore. At least I'm far enough away that the waves aren't as severe, I can turn over and float, try to avoid panic.

What was that story about the little girl whose Daddy told her to be careful of the undertow, but she thought he said Undertoad, so she was afraid of a giant frog in the water waiting for her like a boogie man under the bed. She imagined that it would shoot its long tongue and grab her like an insect. She wouldn't go near the water for years after; I wish I wouldn't have because now...the Undertoad has me.

I can float for a long time, surely someone will see me. Larry and Diane are in the palapa reading. Don't they realize I'm in trouble, haven't they missed me yet? I can't even see the palapa, how far have I floated, how long have I been out here? At least twenty minutes.

I panic again, oh my God, swim hard for shore, harder, oh Lord. I'm wearing myself out. I'll pray; oh, you hypocrite! I'll pray anyway, it can't hurt. Lord, please help me, I promise I will believe in you and not be a sinner. I'm not that bad a sinner anyway. Oh Christ, what a double-dealer I am. What's the matter with me, don't give up, just keep floating, block negative thoughts and think positive. I'm positive I am going to die.

Think logically, once Larry figures out I'm missing he'll go into the restaurant, raise a commotion and they'll call the Salvavidas. Then they'll get a boat or Jet Ski and come find me; that's plausi-

ble. I'm rested again, I'll try and break free, swim hard, wait for a wave to help me toward shore. Now, swim... harder, Go, Go.

Jesus Christ! I'm getting further away from shore. Don't fight it, roll over and float again, and breathe, for God's sake; don't panic. I'm not dying, I haven't heard God's voice or seen any Angels, my life hasn't flashed before my eyes; this isn't dying. I'm just in danger of dying, in grave danger. Is there any other kind? Ha, ha! That's good, that's the ticket. I'll think of famous quotes and float on my back, I can float forever.

The sun is incredibly hot, and the atmosphere is bright, surreal like a high plains winter freeze when the air is so frigid that it looks white, but the temperature is 100. Even the hotels look white, blanco, but it's not winter, I think I am hallucinating. I feel sick, Mother always said, "Never go swimming until an hour after you eat, or you'll get cramps and drown." It wasn't 30 minutes ago that I ate and now I am going to drown, you should never argue with a known saying.

"It's not unheard of for a skeptic or agnostic to think in religious terms," my professor 50 years ago said that, and he was a renowned sceptic, agnostic and atheist and expert on all religion. He was an ordained minister and an arrogant bastard. There were 50 people in the class; I came in late one time and he called me out in front of everyone, told me I was an inconsiderate buffoon. I wasn't sure what he meant, I assumed it was akin to being a religious heathen. Is this what they mean by my life flashing before my eyes? I had forgotten that embarrassing episode.

Maybe I should look to sea instead of the shore, think outside the box. I'm past the big waves so wait for a swell and when I'm at the top look for a fishing boat; they should be returning to take their catch to the market. Nothing there, and now I grow weary, my muscles are starting to fatigue, and I've swallowed so much salt water. Suddenly I see the reality, I see where this is headed, and it isn't good. I think of my children and hate the thought of them being told that I was lost at sea, presumed drowned, isn't that how the papers describe it?

I should be better prepared for death. Maybe if I were raised according to the Quran or Buddhism or if I were a Hindu or even a Catholic; Presbyterian is what I am, and it seems so inadequate now. I went to bible study every week, Sunday school and church on Sunday, choir practice on Wednesday, and Bible camp in the summer, but right now at this crucial moment all I remember from those 18 years of lessons is how to prepare for a nuclear attack; dive under the pew and bury your head in your hands. What was Reverend Ryerson's lesson about dying, about how to die; I don't remember. We go to heaven, I recollect, but how does it work? I had college courses, but I am not an expert in religious doctrine, like the arrogant professor.

If I were God everyone would live forever, that was a game we used to play: what you would do if you were God, but I remember now, it isn't true; I didn't say that. Living forever wasn't part of my personal God world, I made the same inane comments as everyone else, end world hunger, stop children from suffering, no more wars. Mary Jane Thomas made the comment about living forever but there were so many objections to it, you would get bored, no need to make babies. We made fun of her; she was the only person I knew who had three first names and one of them was a boy's name.

I did say, "That must be why God allows children to suffer, because he's bored, seen so many people come and go that it doesn't mean anything to him anymore, people slaughtered, no big deal, I'll just make some more." I heard my mother's best friend, Irene, talking about that idea and it appealed to me, so I borrowed it. That made Mrs. Thomas very mad. She said I was a religious heathen for talking about God that way and I was embarrassed much like in my freshman religious studies class.

I'm hallucinating, these things happened over 60 years ago. I should open my eyes, but they hurt, I should see where I am. Floating is no problem, but thinking is counterproductive, so I won't think. But this is all wrong, not the way I'm going to die, I just know it. It's all a big lie, I've been swimming here before, how can this be happening? Betrayal, that's what I feel…like when you learn that your mother isn't all powerful, or all knowing, and in fact, she lied to you about certain things. Biff Noonan telling me that there is no Santa and laughing when I expressed dismay. I felt betrayed when I went to Mother asking for the truth, but I could see it in her eyes, so my six-year-old world was rearranged again.

Don't it always seem to go that you don't know what you've got till it's gone. That's a known saying right there, impossible to argue against. Double down on all my problems on shore and I would still take it over this.

I've got to see where I am, keep my head up, wait, I see someone on shore, "Help, help me," I shout as loud as I can and I wave my arms like crazy, "Help, please!" oh no, it's the hat salesman. He has about 10 hats piled on his head, he looks like a deformed cowboy, a long-necked vaquero seeking disoriented cattle on a deserted beach. I am in that absurd Marquis de Sade play; I'm the star.

This is serious now. I need to think, relax and reason through solutions not daydreams. How long have I been here, thirty min-

utes, forty, I'll bet they're mobilizing right now but I don't see anyone. The hotels look like they are moving, and I'm trapped in one spot; is this really an ocean current or is it a rip current created by the hurricane in the Pacific? The waves have been high all summer, the equatorial current is further out to sea, but this is a living, breathing creature that holds me, suspended in its womb.

What the hell difference does it make, I can't get out of it, what am I supposed to do, swim against it, with it? That seems to make sense, I tried to swim against it and got worn out, but I feel fine now.

"Señor!"

I am at peace with myself and this situation. I resolve to....
"Señor!"

What was that? God's talking to me and he's a Mexican. I need to leave word, but how, the secret to life has been revealed just when I'm going to die, and no one will be the wiser. Of course, I'm in Mexico and God is everything to all people, it stands to reason.

"*Señor, agarra la boya.*" Grab the buoy...what a strange thing to be saying. Then I see him, a vision I swear on the bible, is shrouded in a radiant light, like a sun beam. He swims toward me, a *Mazatlán Salvavida*, 'Un *guardia que salva la vida*', a lifeguard.

He tossed the buoy toward me and backed off quickly in case I'm in a panic, which I'm not. Ok, I did panic earlier but not now. I want to talk to him, embrace him, and share my insights but I realize that he's still worried about getting us to shore. Suddenly I feel an amazing sense of relief that quickly turns to a kind of embarrassment. I feel like telling him I'm fine, that I was never in danger. But I clutch the life buoy like a child's teddy bear ready to defend it to the death. The buoy was attached by a tether strapped to his back with a harness of some kind, an umbilical cord stretched from the womb of the current to my mother savior.

Time blurred a bit at this point. I remember him telling me to kick hard then I waited as he surveyed the waves for the right moment to swim and we didn't go straight to shore but diagonally across the breakers. I could feel his power as he pulled me through the waves. We reached the beach; I had difficulty standing plus I was out of breath. He offered his shoulder pantomiming that he would help me, but I shook my head. I felt like flinging myself on the ground to kiss the sand.

"You saved me," I said in English.

"Si," he replied simply, watching me...I realized later to make certain I was ok, but I misinterpreted it to mean that he was expecting something.

He told me, "*La corriente es muy fuerte aquí. Debe tener cuidado y observar las banderas de advertencia.*"

I looked to where he pointed, and the red flag flew meaning don't go swimming. He began to leave, hurriedly jogging back to a 4-wheeler parked at the edge of the sand but there were so many things I wanted to share, feelings to express, yet all I could think of was to repeat, "You saved my life." He smiled and waved.

"*Cuál es tu nombre?*" I yelled after him.

"Eddie," he shouted back.

I felt a tremendous loss as he departed, a sense that I owed him something. Not money, maybe companionship or brotherhood, we were interconnected somehow. I wanted a remembrance of what happened; a picture together on the spot where he rescued me, something I could share with my family and friends back home. I imagined the two of us gazing at the camera as though it were the evil current itself, my arm around him smiling in the face of near disaster. Instead, he roared away searching for other stupid swimmers.

I slowly walked back to the palapa where I expected a hero's welcome, plopped down on the chair, water dripping from my hair into my eyes. I observed my shoes where I had placed them, my wallet peeking out, everything as I'd left it a lifetime ago.

"What happened?" Larry asked, "We saw you talking to the lifeguard."

"Didn't you see him save me?"

"No. I just told Larry that I can't see you in the water."

"We didn't know what you were doing," Larry added.

"I thought that you sent him to find me, he saved my life. I was trapped in the undertow, the rip current." They stared at me, confused.

"You just now missed me? I've been gone forever, an eternity; my whole life flashed before my eyes."

Diane shook her head and displayed her watch, "You went in the water at one o'clock. You were barely gone thirteen minutes."

WILLIAM DARBY

"NEXT CASE," startled William from a deep sleep, or at least he thought it was from a deep sleep. He awakened to discover he was not in bed at all; instead, he was sitting in a small unfamiliar room, no windows, bare walls, and a single uncovered bulb hanging from the ceiling. Yet a most peculiar thing; he was in his pajamas. The pink pajamas with horizontal magenta stripes that he hated because Great Aunt Judy had given them to him under the mistaken belief that he was a girl. But they were the only clean pajamas he could find because Tuesday was not a wash day and mother was strict about her washday schedule. William did not deem it unusual that his mother would wake him from a deep sleep but never with those two words.

Eleven years old, William was not a particularly popular boy; a bit on the chubby side, but not terribly so, he was not too tall and not too short, he was average in a very normal way. William was an inquisitive child and he naturally wondered how he had arrived in this peculiar situation. And peculiar was a word that William enjoyed very much, a word that he had recently discovered. It gave him great pleasure to roll it around in his mouth which is what he was doing when the door suddenly burst open, and an appallingly nervous man rushed into the small room.

"NEXT CASE," he shouted although he and William were alone, and William would have heard him had he whispered.

"I am not deaf, you needn't shout."

Whereupon the nervous little man, wearing what appeared to be a rented tuxedo, his hair straining in every direction but flat, stammered, "Oh my, we're so late, I called you ever so many minutes ago and now you are LATE. Please hurry. We mustn't keep the judges waiting."

"What are you talking about?" William asked.

"YOUR CASE," he shouted, pulling on William's arm across a well-lit hallway where many people were gawking at them. The flustered man opened a large double door and pushed William inside before he could say any of the things that were going through his mind and a great many things were occupying William's mind at that moment, not the least of which was that this was a most peculiar situation. He was so preoccupied that he failed to notice anything of the large room in which he had been so forcefully injected, until finally he became aware that many eyes were staring at him in an intense manner.

A court reporter, a large lady with a beehive hairdo that seemed at least two feet high and glasses so big that the lenses looked like magnifying glasses, held her hands poised over an old-fashioned typewriter. She was staring at William, keenly, as though her entire life was devoted to what he might say.

Because of his exemplary upbringing, William greeted her, "Hello," he nodded politely, and the lady typed. The staccato clicks of five letters roared in the room.

"How are you?" William asked as a test to see what would happen and the machine gun click of eleven letters echoed. He decided not to say anything more in favor of trying to determine what kind of situation he faced.

"I must be dreaming," he mumbled. The relentless pounding of the typewriter reminded him of his vow of silence. He took the quiet moment to look about. There before him on a huge wooden platform sat two very large, ominous judges in black robes, one was a very black man, and one was a very white man, but they were both of sophisticated and regal bearing who looked down upon William with a questioning and disapproving (at least in William's mind) gaze.

"Bailiff read the charges, if you please."

The disheveled bailiff, the man who had awoken him so rudely, began: "The case of Billy Derby V the State, charged with avarice..." at this a gasp went up from the courtroom. "Gluttony, lust."

'NO' shouted from the back of the room. The jury shuffled uneasily in the box. "....Sloth and pride, but worst of all, lying to his mother." Several onlookers fainted dead away.

"I am not Billy Derby, I am William Darby."

"He seems like such a nice boy doesn't he, Reginald?" The white judged asked of his colleague.

"Yes, Warren, I agree but he's somewhat out of touch," Reginald leaned back in his chair hands tented to his chin in a solemn, knowing manner.

"Excuse me your honors," William interrupted and the judges both stopped and peered down at him, "I think that I am lost.".

"Where were you going?" Warren asked.

"I don't know," William countered.

"How can you be lost if you don't know where you're going?" Reginald questioned him suspiciously.

"Perhaps you were coming here. Then, you see, you wouldn't be lost at all," Judge Warren suggested.

"I don't believe so because I'm not really certain where I am. You see, I was in my bed the last I remember and now, I am here."

"We are all here," Reginald indicated others in the courtroom.

"What is it that you want?" Warren asked. A question that confused William terribly.

"I don't want anything."

"You must be more specific, Billy."

"William!"

"Reginald, or Your Honor."

"No, your honor, Reginald, my name is William Darby."

"No, it's Billy Derby," Warren countered.

"I know my own name," William insisted.

"OBJECTION," a large man sitting at a table to Williams's right stood glowering at him.

"Who are you," William asked?

"Prosecuting attorney, and I object your honor." The prosecutor was an old man his long narrow face creased with the ravages of time, wearing a dark suit with a checkered vest and a watch on a long chain which he occasionally took out and consulted then swirled menacingly around and around. His voice was gruff, and he spoke in huffs and puffs and he very strangely resembled a ferret.

"On what grounds do you object?" Reginald asked.

"On the coffee grounds of preposterosity. The happy-hunting grounds of alienation of appallations and aliasing without proper introspection; PLUS, intensification of legal la te dadeda." He strolled meaningfully to the jury box and with a disdainful look pointed at William, "He mocks the court with mockdoodle and fainwaingle lying and lowing and confuscating all that is lawful, and he is scornful of the very lawyers that this land sits for, It is a travelocity of jurisprudence."

The jury, comprised of a rainbow of citizens, men and women, all older than the prosecutor, in their wheelchairs and walkers, bellowed and applauded causing the judges to shout simultaneously, "Order in the courtroom."

The prosecutor bowed to the jury and threw kisses to the audience. Once again, he approached William pointing at him menacingly, "The defendant, seemless as an innocensed child, but he is coldly villainaneous, desicated to moral wrongdoing." He wiped a tear from his eye then used the handkerchief to blow his nose.

He gathered himself before the grand finale, "This boy is charged with falsehhooding the very mother of his birthright who sprang him from the womb of truthfulness and light. This is a darkened boy of evil intentsifications. You must find him not innocent as charged."

There was pandemonium in the courtroom, cheering and shouting. The judges pounded their large gavels furiously.

"I object to the objection," intoned a small voice from William's left and everyone stopped.

William spoke up quickly, "Who are you," surprised to find a slight girl with big black eyes and pigtails, sucking on a lollipop?

"Your defense attorney, of course, and by the way, nice pj's."

"But...but, you're just a little girl, you look like you're seven."

'Eight actually, but my mother says I'm precocious."

"On what grounds do you object," asked Warren.

"I site the case of Brown v the Board 1874, irrelevant and immaterial," she stated knowingly. "And the case of right v wrong, year one, and the case of Cain v Able, year 20, the question was asked and answered, your honor. He states that his name is William Darby. I move to strike from the record."

"No!" The court reporter flung herself upon the typewriter.

"Excellent argument councilor," Warren applauded.

"Overruled," Reginald instructed.

The typewriter clicked with the rhythm of an electric sewing machine. William stood quietly as his defense attorney played with her dolls and the prosecutor snored at his table. The jury seemed preoccupied with their medical ailments and were ignoring the proceedings entirely.

The judges alone watched him intently. "He seems a bit slow, don't you think, Warren?"

"Yes, I must agree with you, Reginald."

William spoke, surprising everyone, "I know the problem, your honors, Reginald and Warren, sirs. You see, I know Billy Derby, he is a friend of mine, but he lives on East Main and I live on West Main."

"You really must be more specific, Bill"

"I don't understand."

"He really is slow, Warren, perhaps we should have him evaluated by the psychiatrist."

"What is your address, specifically," Warren asked.

"133 West Main."

"More specific."

"Osage Village, Missouri"

"More," Reginald urged.

"America," William said hesitating a bit.

The defense attorney put her dolls down and came to the witness box and whispered in his ear, "He means what planet."

"Oh, well, um uh....Earth"

A moan went up from the audience, the prosecutor jumped to his feet and shouted, "The prosecution rests."

"That would explain a lot wouldn't it, Reginald?"

"Yes, Warren, I believe that this justifies the psychiatric evaluation. The court is in recess for 30 minutes while the evaluation proceeds."

"Oh goody, recess," the little girl said.

"All rise," the bailiff shouted.

As soon as the judges retired, the audience, jury, and everyone else rushed out pushing and shoving, the elderly ricocheting off the ambulatory with their wheelchairs, scattering people wildly. William was alone.

"Hello, Bill, how's the trial going?"

"My name is William, who are you?"

"Harold Long, Governor of this wonderful Island. You look a bit down, things not going your way? You have a damn good team working for you, keep your spirits up, lad. I was in the neighborhood, thought I would stop by and see how the proceedings are...., well," he said with a chuckle...., "proceeding."

"They think I committed a crime."

"Oh, no, Bill. We did away with crime a long time ago. This has to do with morality and political consequences. It's the idea that the process is more important than the result." He put his arm around William and walked him to a window. They watched the little girl playing hopscotch, the jury playing tag in their wheelchairs and walkers, others in a game of kickball and the judges on a teeter-totter.

"You see Judge Reginald there, his father was a judge and his father and so on, now what would Reginald do if we did away with the courts? We have to have trials, or the entire system will collapse."

"But I'm not who they think I am. I'm William Darby not Billy Derby. I know Billy and he's kind of mean."

"Oh, it doesn't really matter, does it, Bill? My understanding is that Billy Derby lied to his mother and that's what this is about. I'll bet you lied to your mother somewhere along the line so what does it matter if you are getting tried for an old lie or Billy is getting tried for a new one. Remember, it's the process that's important, not the end result. Everyone is entitled to a fair trial by a jury of their peers whether you did anything wrong or not. And that is what you are getting."

William watched the jury of his peers asleep in their wheelchairs and on the park benches with their walkers lying at their feet. The little girl waved at him.

"It matters to me," William said quietly.

"Look Bill, Dr. Clara is here."

Dr. Clara was a clown. At least she was wearing clown make-up with a red fuzzy wig and bright red nose.

"Hello Billy, we need to get to it. We only have about twenty minutes."

"But you're a clown."

"What a rude thing to say. Didn't your mother teach you any manners, young man? That is one mark against you right there. Now, here is a picture, what does it look like to you? And remember there aren't any right or wrong answers."

"It looks like a lady with no shirt and her boobs are showing."

She wrote in her notebook and said out loud, "Obsessed with sex."

"But that's what the picture is," he protested.

"Let me see that. Darn, how did that get in there? Never mind about the pictures. Ok, I'm going to say a word and you say the first thing that pops into your mind. Ok, here we go, black."

"Dark"

"No, not dark, you should say white or night, but not dark."

"I thought you said there are no right or wrong answers."

"Don't argue. Ok, here's the next word. Sun"

"Daughter"

"No, not son like a child, sun like the star. Ok try one more word and please think about it first, try to get it correct. Right."

"Left."

"No, the answer is wrong, you didn't get any correct."

"ALL RISE"

The judges entered, took their seats very dignified; the audience stood quietly as did the jury who fascinated William because they were no longer the old and infirm but young adults with tattoos and piercings and multi-colored hair and clothes.

"Please be seated," Reginald instructed.

The bailiff announced, "Court Psychiatrist, Dr. Clara please come forward. Place your right hand on the bible. Do you swear...."

"I most certainly do not."

"Take your seat in the witness box."

Reginald instructed her, "Dr. Clara please present your findings to the court."

Dr. Clara honked her bicycle horn twice, "After a complete and thorough evaluation it is my finding that the defendant is rude and unsociable. He is obsessed with sex and has a very low IQ, borderline socially non-functional, a psychopath and schizophrenic. He doesn't know the difference between right and wrong."

Judge Warren interrupted her and said, "So you are saying that..."

"Exactly so, your honor, he is perfectly normal, in every way, and competent to stand trial."

"Thank you, Dr. Clara that will be all," Reginald dismissed the court psychiatrist. "Prosecution please present your summary."

The little girl who was now on Williams right stood and said, "This is a difficult case because of the defendant's age, but the case...."

"Wait," William shouted, "I thought she was my attorney."

"Order in the court," Warren shouted. "Please continue counselor."

She stuck her tongue out at William then continued, "As I was saying, the case history is quite clear especially, Scopes v Tennessee, 1925, which proved that the word of God trumps the word of man."

A murmur rose from the crowd. "Lynch the little liar," shouted a man from the back of the room.

"AND, the case of Smith v Wesson, 1917, that the best way to cure a liar is at the point of a gun, plus the fact that he is from earth," she said while putting a new dress on her doll. "The prosecution rests your honor."

The audience roared with approval. "Off with his head, throw the book at him," were just a few of the epitaphs shouted.

"Order in the court," Warren yelled while Reginald pounded his gavel.

"Attorney for the defense, your summary please."

A small dark-haired man with a large moustache stood and addressed the jury who seemed totally disinterested, "Damas y caballeros de la corte. Mi estimado cliente..."

"Wait," shouted William, "who is he?"

"He's your attorney."

"Well, what happened to the other guy, I can't understand this one?"

"It doesn't matter, Bill. We couldn't understand the other one."

So, the defense attorney continued his summation in Spanish while the Judges, jury, audience and Prosecuting Attorney all occupied themselves in various ways. When he was finished, he bowed to the jury and sat down giving William a thumbs up and a big smile. It was some moments before the judges noticed that the summation was over. The court reporter watched William, with her hands poised.

William said, "This is crazy, isn't it?" She typed furiously those 18 characters then watched him closely for more.

William sighed and sat in an empty chair in the jury box. He wondered if he would ever get home, "I must be asleep and dreaming all this."

"Dude, I wish I was. This is totally boring," a girl of about 19 with pink hair and a ring in her nose agreed.

"What happened to the other jury."

"Couldn't tell you, I was just in the park with some friends and that Dude," she pointed at the bailiff, "came and said I had to be on the jury and hurry up and he was all pulling on my arm and everything. He is totally wasted on something."

"What do you think will happen to me?"

"I don't know, like, I guess you'll grow up and be a postman or something."

"I mean about the trial."

"Haven't got a clue. I don't pay attention to lame stuff like that. But I will give you a little advice." She leaned close to his ear and whispered, "Lose the pajamas. They're just not you; you know what I mean?"

"My great aunt Judy gave them to me. She thinks I'm a girl." She raised her eyebrows at him.

"They're my only clean ones," William suddenly felt very depressed.

"Well, I'm just saying. I think you're an ok kid and I'm gonna' vote not guilty."

Reginald pounded his gavel, "Ladies and gentlemen of the jury, you have heard the testimony presented here today. It is your job to find Billy Derby innocent....," and the audience laughed uproariously, causing Warren to bang his gavel loudly, "....or guilty, as you deem proper in your capacity as 12 jurors, good and true, patrons of the Goddess of Justice and all that is fair and righteous...."

"Oh my God, yada, yada. Is he ever going to finish?" The pink-haired girl whispered to William. "I've got a lot of stuff to do."

"....and so the jury will retire to the deliberation room and debate all of the evidence presented here today. When you have reached a unanimous verdict, you will return to the courtroom and render that verdict along with your recommendation for sentencing. Bailiff, if you please."

"ALL RISE," the bailiff announced. The Judges exited as did the jury. The audience filed out slowly along with the other members of the court except for the court reporter who sat watching William intently. He thought about running back to the unfamiliar room where he awoke that morning, which seemed like years ago. But before he could act, the bailiff, shouted, ALL RISE and the jury filed back into the jury box followed closely by the judges. They hadn't been gone 30 seconds.

"Will the defendant stand and face the jury. Has the jury reached a unanimous decision?"

"Yes, your honor....,"

"Wait, stop the presses and hold your horses, WAIT, your honor,"

"What in the world...," Reginald pounded his gavel.

"What is all of that commotion?" Warren demanded.

"Your honors," the bailiff rushed into the room, his disheveled hair flying in all directions, out of breath and screaming, "there has been a terrible mistake, your honors, members of the jury, I present to you the REAL Billy Derby. That boy," he pointed at William, "is an imposter. This is the real Billy Derby," he brought into the room a boy of Williams age with red hair and bright blue eyes who was obviously surprised and distraught until he saw William standing in the room. He burst into a smile and waved at his friend, "William, William, WILLIAM."

William opened his eyes to find his mother shaking him. "What is wrong with you? You look like something the cat drug in. Didn't you sleep last night?"

"Oh, Mom, it's really you," he grabbed his mother and hugged her.

"Do you have a fever? What have you done? Why are you acting this way?"

"Nothing, I just had a bad dream. I can't wait to go to school. I love school, no scratch that, I can't lie, I don't love it, but I want to go, I want everything to be normal."

His mother felt his forehead, looked at his throat, took his temperature and fussed over him until she was certain he was not sick. "What was your bad dream? "

William told her that it was about telling a lie.

"Did you tell a lie?"

He told her that he had not, at least not the one that he was accused of in the dream.

"Well, maybe there's a lesson somewhere in that dream."

William hurried through breakfast, was dressed and ready for school. He couldn't wait to find Billy Derby and tell him about the bad dream and the part that Billy had played. William knew he would laugh at him but didn't care, he had to tell someone.

"Where's Billy," he asked Billy's sister, Peggy?

"I don't know. He wasn't in his room this morning. I think he ran away because he got in trouble for lying to Momma. I'm sure he'll be back soon."

William dropped his lunch sack, put his head in his hands, "No, I don't think he will."

JOHN THE PREACHER

L ast week I chanced upon a man downtown, a man that I assumed was a vagrant, while he, in turn, believed that I was an angel. How he made such a mistake is worth explaining, mainly to preserve his memory, although neither of us was correct in our assumption.

This man, named John, was sitting on a bench on Congress Avenue. The weather was especially cold for Austin, Texas even in December. There weren't many people out that frigid night. Light from a streetlamp illuminated his poorly clad figure and I sensed that he was watching as Barbara and I walked by, causing me to hesitate a moment with the wariness that we have for suspicious strangers. He was thin with a full head of white hair, a stubbly grey face and vacant eyes that bespoke a long time without creature comforts. His knees were drawn to his chest as he rocked slowly, muttering a dialogue that I couldn't understand. I could see his breath in the strangely cold Texas air.

Barbara was urging me to hurry and finally came back to tug at my arm because we were late for the performance, *A Tuna Christmas* at the Paramount with Jaston Williams and Joe Sears, although it was our third time seeing it. The actors change the lines each year to make the material fresh and up to date, so I wasn't bored. I quickly forgot the old man on the bench outside the theatre.

Monday was again overcast and grey in Austin as I hurried to meet some friends for a business lunch in the Colorado Street Cafe. John was standing by a trash can in front of the restaurant. I remembered him from the night of the play although he was taller than I would have thought, taller than my 6'1." I put my hand in my pocket as I drew abreast, he took my actions for a handout, "I don't want your money, Bobby," he said. Startled I stopped short and looked at him, but before I could speak my guests arrived and we hurried into the restaurant. John had a deep voice, totally inconsistent with what I expected, not the voice of a bum or at least how I imagined a bum to sound. Maybe he said, 'I don't want your money, Buddy', still, it sounded so clear, I was certain he used my name.

I hurried through the soup and made some lame excuses and vague promises of calling in a day or two and rushed out into the frigid air, but he wasn't there. My route back to the car was south to Seventh Street then east toward Congress. He was sitting on the same bench in front of the theater, head down, chin on chest, eyes closed, "Are you an angel?" he said. I waited thinking that he was having a conversation with himself, a habit that I assumed all vagrants' practice.

"I think that you are an angel," he said, this time looking at me. He wore khaki pants with a blue checked lumberjack shirt and a thin windbreaker unbuttoned; his face was gaunt and grey as the sky. The most remarkable thing about him was his voice, that and thick white hair like a luminous halo. For some reason I imagined him to be a preacher fallen from grace; drunken on the pulpit preaching a sermon, slurring words, the congregation gasping in disgust, the Elders whispering and gesturing, vowing to deal with him harshly this time.

"Say, how do you know my name, old timer," I said loudly. I'd never in my life called anyone 'old timer.'

"I don't know you," he replied, shaking his head as though he was disappointed.

"But you said, 'I don't want your money, Bobby.' How do you know my..."

His deep voice boomed, "Without faith it is impossible to please God."

"What?" I asked, trying to understand.

"Dead is our personal life, were it even the noblest, finest, and most pious, when it does not have its beginnings in the fear of God," he said, looking into my eyes, giving me a chill beyond the weather; I turned and walked away.

"Don't you understand?" he shouted, but I didn't stop, it was all I could do to go to church on Easter Sunday, the last thing I needed was to be preached at by a vagrant in the middle of Congress Avenue during the coldest day of the year. He was still watching when I looked back from the end of the street. I called Barbara from the car phone and asked if she remembered seeing him the night of the play.

"Did you have a drink before you talked to him," she asked?

"Not before lunch," I lied. "I'm sure he said 'Bobby.'" I didn't want to talk about the drinks, an uncomfortable topic between us.

"Why didn't you stay and talk to him?" she said. "He's probably just some crazy old homeless person, go back and ask him who he is and how he knows you because that part bothers me. But please don't start feeling sorry for him and give him money or, God forbid, bring him home. I have to take Camille to Foley's to exchange the dress your mother gave her. Call me later and tell me what happened."

Seemed like sound advice to me, so I turned around at Sixth and Mopac and drove back downtown. He was in the same place and looked at me when I drove past the second time searching for a parking spot. People scurried around ignoring him pointedly. I parked in a fifteen-minute commercial zone, slammed the car door as I got out, feeling foolish about the whole thing. The sky was clinging to the top of One American Center, First City Center and all the other tall buildings, a cold drizzle stung my face as I sat down next to him, "What do you need from me, Partner," I immediately regretted the condescending attitude.

"People scurry away like roaches in the light when I share the Truth," he responded. "The Lord's word is a source of ridicule. Thomas Hobbs said, "the only article of faith, which the scriptures maketh simply necessary to salvation is this, that Jesus is Christ. That is the fundamental article of Christian faith," he stopped and wiped the rain from his eyes.

"Why are you telling me this, are you a preacher, do you need some help," I asked? He seemed coherent and his voice was calming.

"I thought that you knew," he replied.

"But I don't."

"When I was a boy, my daddy would bring me to Austin on Saturdays and Sundays from our home in Temple. Daddy would stand on a box in Peace Park and preach the gospel, the nights were hot, but the sun on Sunday, in July, would melt the devil right out of your soul," he stopped to see if I was paying attention.

"People would come from all around to listen, Daddy was a powerful preacher. The colored folk, the poor whites, Mexican workers and their families, every one of them shouting 'amen' and 'hallelujah.' Oh, they would hit their knees when Daddy prayed for them." He smiled as he recollected the memory.

"Then he would say to me, 'pass the plate now, John,' and I would take my hat, hold it out to the flock, and they would give what they could because Daddy gave them hope of a better life.. A ray of hope for all God's children; he was 6'4" and his voice would roar down as if from the heavens above."

John stood and faced me, intimidating as he towered above me, his voice, clear and deep, echoed off the tall buildings around us and the clouds seemed to draw down until they coiled about his white head like a wreath. The rain dribbled down his face like tears on a marble statue.

"There are some among you who remain proud and arrogant in spite of certain knowledge of the absolute truth, there are some of you who have given yourselves over to Satan entirely; for you, hell is voluntary and ever consuming. You will be tortured by your choice for you have cursed yourselves, cursing God and life. You live upon your own vindictive pride like a starving man in the desert, sucking blood out of his own body, but you are never satisfied, and you refuse forgiveness, you curse the true God who calls you. You cannot behold the living God without hatred, and you cry out that the God of life should be annihilated, that God should destroy himself and His own creation."

John began shouting as he leaned over me with his face just inches away, "Repent for our God is a consuming fire and you will burn in the fire of your own wrath for ever and ever and you will yearn for death and annihilation, but you will not attain death, instead you shall burn in hell for all eternity."

The few people on the street hurried away, avoiding us, which was all right with me. John stopped suddenly and crumbled onto the bench beside me, seemingly exhausted, his eyes had taken a fierce glow during his sermon and his beautiful voice had mesmerized me like no Easter Sunday preacher before.

He continued, but calmly, "Daddy would be arrested if he were alive and preaching today."

"Do I know your family or something," I asked him?

He paused breathing deeply, "You think this weather is God's work?" He turned his face to the grey sky. "This is the nasty cold spit of the devil; old Satan is trying to freeze God right out of my soul."

I took a deep breath and pulled him by the arm into a back booth at Serrano's next door to the Theatre, the restaurant was almost empty, "Let's get a cup of coffee," I urged. The waiter looked at me when he asked what we wanted. I thought that John must be hungry, "Do you want something to eat," I asked.

"No, the Lord will provide food for my soul and it's my soul that is wanting, not my body." He wrapped his windbreaker around his chest and leaned against the wall with his knees up to his chin as I had seen him that first night. He continued without any prompt from me, "I was in the Air Force and settled near Colorado Springs, we were so happy, the children, Mary and Larry, of course, they're older now with children of their own. He began rocking again, I thought that he was in physical pain, embarrassed, I looked to see if someone I know might be watching.

"Julian, my wife, she is...was the kindest woman that ever graced God's green earth, not just to me and the kids but to everyone, a pillar of the community and a saint to the schools. She was a comfort and joy to strangers and friends alike, served on all kinds of committees, she was the definition of good. Never an unkind word, always cheering those who were down-trodden, first in line to volunteer at school or church. I loved her more than life itself," he paused, looking at me, and then the coffee as it was set on the table. He didn't drink but wrapped his boney hands around the cup, gripping it to his chest as if trying to ward off a cold wind that penetrated the walls and blew on him alone.

"She had all of the Christian virtues except that she didn't believe in God. When we first met, I assumed she was a devout Christian, she went to church every Sunday. Then as time went on, I thought that she believed in God, but she just didn't like him much."

I laughed thinking John had made a joke, but he was sincere, "Why did she go to Church if she didn't believe in God?" I asked.

"She was a staunch defender of the Church. 'People need their faith,' she would say, but she was adamant that the message of the Church should be teaching of proper values and behavior and not threats about damnation and the wrath of God. She always said that God must be real insecure if he needs everyone to keep praising him all the time. What kind of God would say that he was a jealous god and would visit the iniquity of the Father on the children unto the third and fourth generation of them that hate him?"

"God said that?" I asked, "In reference to what?" He ignored my question.

"I knew that she didn't have faith, but I lived with it. That might surprise you but it's the truth; Mary, our daughter, knew it. Mary's a lot like her mother, they're both well read, intelligent women. Julian taught high school for 30 years, she read the classics and modern books, could quote the bible with anyone, a lot better than the minister who took over the church last year. He and Julian never got along."

John began to chuckle as he told this anecdote, the first sign of passion that I witnessed in him. "We were having a discussion of the parable of Abraham and Isaac. The Preacher lectured long and brilliantly of the symmetry and beauty of Abraham's journey and his unfailing sense of Duty to God; the superhuman act of faith as he prepared his son for sacrifice, our Preacher read the appropriate versus then waited for comments from the class. Julian said 'you know the first time I read that particular passage I pictured God as Groucho Marx jumping out from behind the bush saying Abraham, baby, you should see the look on your face, come on, Abe, I was just fooling, you didn't think I meant it about sacrificing the Kid did you? Get it 'kid' I got the goat right here behind the bush.' Julian could do a great Groucho Marx imitation and the class laughed but not the new Preacher, he just glared at her."

I had a blank look on my face, "I'm sorry," I said, "I am not much up on my bible verses anymore."

"It doesn't matter," he sighed, "I always believed that my faith was strong enough for both of us, strong enough to carry us to eternal life together, that's what physical life is all about you know. Do you recall what Marguerite asked Faust, 'Tell me, how do you stand to religion?' Well, I was Marguerite to Julian's Faust, 'I don't want to affect any belief with my own' she would say, 'Every person needs a spiritual confessor and believing in God is as good as any.' That was her philosophy and it served us for many years."

I started to say that I didn't know who Marguerite and Faust were, but he didn't wait for my response, he was drinking coffee and talking without my prompts anyway, so I let the story flow. It occurred to me that maybe I could help him in some way, that our meeting might be more than chance.

"Through the years I gradually came to understand her better. Her philosophy evolved as she grew more learned, I don't mean that it changed, just that it became more concise, and she believed with all her heart that there is no God. I used to ask her, 'What happens when we're dead.'

'Nothing,' she said, 'nothing at all. Why does that frighten you so? We're like the leaves of trees that fall to the earth, each leaf is replaced by another, no reincarnation, no heaven, no hell, no burst of light, no consciousness at all, just the end. I don't understand why that upsets people so much,' she told me. So, I asked her who's making all this happen, surely you don't suggest that it's blind chance. She would laugh and give me a hug, 'John, there's no plan in the sky, like a God business plan where he checks his books each day, each second, and pronounces that this sheep will be born, that person shall have a heart attack, an earthquake in California, a war in Israel; John, these things happen according to the natural function of our weather and the internal dynamics of our planet, people die because their bodies fail them or some idiot murders them, not because of the whims of a supernatural being."

The waiter refilled our cups, I thought he looked relieved that John wasn't shouting anymore, "Was she an unhappy person?" I asked.

"She was the happiest most contented person I've ever known; she brought joy and laughter to everyone around her."

"Why did you stay together so long if you were so different?"

"Oh, Bobby, I loved that woman. You've got to understand, what I'm telling you evolved over 53 years. As a young man courting, I was blinded by her beauty and energy, she was tall with brown hair and eyes bluer than the sky, I loved her so much. I ached all over when we were apart, I couldn't have cared less if she believed in God or not. Nothing would have changed if Gordon Pecant hadn't come along, we would have gone on with our lives forever."

Then he started to preach again, "Though he, or an angel from heaven, preach any other gospel unto you let him be accursed. Those who do not come to Jesus Christ shall not be among the chosen, I believe that with all my heart. Do you understand what all that means?" He asked me.

"I don't understand, John, who is Gordon Pecant?"

John breathed deeply and scowled at me, a frightening look, and said, "He's the filthy, wicked scum that murdered our twelve-year-old grandson."

"Oh," I said wishing horribly that I wouldn't have asked. Maybe I wouldn't be able to solve this man's problems after all.

"He's a horrible man, the epitome of evil. Julian was a flower in sunlight. He was a cold fungus in the dark. The filthy animal gloried in telling the gruesome details about his crimes, much of it was made up, but one thing is for sure, he killed our boy. He told the police where to find the body, of course, that was after he had described every perverted thing that he'd done to him." John put his head on the table and cried, gross sucking sobs that rose from his gut like the whine of a pump sucking air instead of water. I didn't even have the decency to put my hand out to him, just hunkered back in the booth and pulled my coat lapels higher around my ears. I scowled at a couple in the booth across from us and they left. We'd cleared everyone out of our section. Finally, I was able to put my hand on his arm, "John, I'm so sorry."

He continued to cry but softly, "Then after the trial Pecant found God," John said derisively, "There is no sin, and there can be no sin on all of the earth which the Lord will not forgive to the truly repentant. Pecant announced that he'd found forgiveness in the arms of the Lord. I'll never forget what he said, 'without faith it is impossible to please God for he that cometh to God must believe that he is, and that he is a rewarder of them that diligently seek him." John looked at me as I stared blankly. "That's from Hebrews," he explained.

"Then Pecant said 'I'm here before you today to show that I have repented my sins and I embrace all that is good and holy, to prove it here is a written record of my sins and where you can find the bodies of the poor unfortunate souls who were my victims when I was the consort of the Devil and now I bow before the one and only true Prince of Heaven."

"Did you believe him," I asked?

"Julian claimed that it was bogus, but it isn't my place to forgive him or not. That's God's business, I left it to Him to decide, but not Julian, she ranted and raved and organized the community to demand the death sentence. She said the goody two shoes could leave it to God if they wanted but she was going to make sure the murderer wouldn't hurt anyone else in this life."

"She must have been successful," I said.

"Yes, but it split our community terribly, a small influential group opposed the death sentence and Julian attacked them as well as the murderer; unfortunately, the Preacher was among them. Preacher said that we should all praise God for helping the evil man find faith and realize the error of his ways, he went on and on about God's incredible fountain of forgiveness. Well, Julian couldn't take it anymore, she jumped up and started down the aisle, muttering and crying, getting angrier by the second. 'Bullshit' she called out, 'my grandson is dead. Nothing is going to bring him back and the bastard who did it deserves to die. He's a liar and murderer and you're treating him like a saint.'

"When she got to the door she turned and shouted, 'there is no God you idiot' then she ran out. I was following behind wanting to comfort her, frankly I thought the Preacher was way out of line. I guess that she thought of something else because she stopped and started back. She saw me coming and looked into my eyes and said 'I'm so sorry, John,' then turned and ran down the steps but she slipped on the ice and hit her head on the iron rail, she died right there in the snow with her head in my lap."

I felt like I couldn't breathe. John stared at his coffee cup, finally he took a drink, "Everyone gathered around looking down at us. That idiot Preacher said, 'she didn't mean it she was just tired,' but she meant every word." John started crying again.

"He that shall blaspheme against the Holy Ghost, shall never have forgiveness, but shall be guilty of an everlasting sin, don't you see yet what it means, Bobby," he sobbed, "Don't you understand yet?"

I felt out of my element and wished that Barbara could help me. She understood people better than me. But I thought maybe I did understand, at least what it meant to him and the torment created in his mind.

"At her funeral the Preacher didn't mention what she said. He and everyone else believed that Julian had cracked under the pressure of working on the death sentence committee and losing her grandson. When he put the dirt on her coffin and said, 'God grant Julian her rightful spot in the Kingdom of Heaven,' I really broke down, Mary and I both knew that Mother believed with all her heart that there is no God; I was afraid for her and for me because I believe with all my heart that there is. I was going to be with God in heaven and Julian, my beautiful, good, kind Julian was going to burn in hell because she denied God's existence yet the evil one was going to go to heaven because he had embraced God and recanted his sins."

"John, I don't think that's the way it works," I protested feebly, my glaring lack of knowledge contributed to a broken-down response to a poor man who needed help, I just flat didn't know what to do, he believed everything he said, and his bible upbringing was going to destroy him.

"Back home after the service I was just lost, the house seemed so empty. Mary said that I was a fool to have the new Preacher handle mother's service when she hated him so and Mother didn't believe in God anyway. My son, Larry heard her and started screaming at her, "What in the hell are you talking about," he shouted, "Dad what's this all about?"

"That was in November. I sat around the house for a while then went to the bus station, didn't tell anyone where I was going, just wanted to come back to where my Daddy preached, maybe try and understand it all, to see if I would receive a sign. But all I find here are these tall buildings and the foul stench of the devil slobbering on my face every time I look up to heaven, God is still testing me and I'm about to fail."

John banged the table with his fist startling me and the waiter who was walking by, again I searched for something to say, "John, surely God will let Julian into heaven. Listen, come home with me and we'll get you cleaned up and contact your children. They must be frantic looking for you," I spoke slowly, not really knowing where I was going with it.

He looked at me and then started crying again, "You're not an angel, are you Bobby, do you even believe in God?"

"Yes, I do John, but I haven't thought about it a lot, I used to go to Church all the time, just not much lately."

"Do you know if your wife believes in God," He asked.

"I'm sure she does, John, why's that important?"

"I thought that you were an angel."

"I know you did, but why?" I pleaded.

"When I was sitting on that bench praying for a sign from God, you materialized out of the darkness like an Angel of Mercy, just swooped out of the night and appeared before me in my hour of need, then someone said, 'come on Bobby, you'll make us late.' My grandson's name was Bobby and that's what Julian and I would say to him every Sunday on the way to Church, 'Come on Bobby, you'll make us late,' I thought you must be an angel sent by the Lord to help me."

My first instinct was to apologize but I waited, neither of us had much more to say. I wanted so badly to be able to help him, we sat there in the back booth of a Mexican restaurant both of us hoping for a sign from God. Finally, John said, "There's only one way for me to join Julian. I've known the answer all along. I can't sit next to that evil Pecant in Heaven while the finest woman who ever lived sleeps with the devil in Hell."

He didn't seem angry any longer, just stood and started for the door much faster than I could have imagined. I jumped up and stumbled into the waiter, "Can I get you folks anything else," he asked obviously relieved that we were leaving.

Fumbling in my pocket for change took a while as all I had was bills, "John stop," I called out. I threw some bills on the table but didn't wait for the waiter to return. I ran outside and slipped on the ice that had formed, falling hard on my backside, with images in my mind of joining Julian in ignoble death on the sidewalk. After struggling to my feet, I walked around the block then went back to my car shivering, sore and discouraged.

I tried to call Barbara, but she wasn't home. I called my office but didn't have any messages. So, I sat on the bench in front of the Paramount, waited about twenty minutes then moved under an awning in front of the camera store. The weather was worsening, getting colder and it was starting to snow, I didn't feel much like an Angel. I wish that I would have given John my coat, but I never saw him again.

PAPYRUS GONOLEK

In Africa there exists a tribe of people where, when a baby is born, the relatives on both sides of the family all come to meet the newborn. Grandmothers, aunts and uncles, cousins and all the neighbors line up for their turn to introduce themselves. Each says something like 'Hello Zaire, my name is Adana and I am your second cousin on your mother's side.' So as Zaire grows older, he learns everyone's name and the names of all the babies that come after. Thus, a great big, beautiful family of relatives and friends is built into their culture right from birth.

Now, that part is important to the story but not the most important part. This just illustrates that for a thousand years these people have a tradition of cooperative family and village relations, and they work things out according to the customs of the tribe relying on a long history of rulings, edicts and proclamations, none of which were written down because they are an ignorant people with no written language. But they were smart enough to remember all the laws, word for word. Remember these people are poor uninformed natives who don't have the benefit of television, telephones, computers, or any such modern necessities that make life worth living. All they have is a great big country full of rivers, mountains, trees, animals, birds and plants plus the moon and stars at night. They are sorely deprived of the conveniences of life.

At this big gathering for the newborn baby, the children play, the mothers' gossip and cook, the teenagers flirt with each other and the elders discuss various things that important people discuss. This particular day, of Zaire's birth, a neighbor by the name of Talib proceeded to tell a story about a man named Lekan from a nearby village. One day Lekan and his sons were hunting not far from the village when they grew weary and rested on a large rock under a Mopane tree. Time to time they would see birds flitting about and, of course, they were interested in observing these actions because many things can be learned from the habits of birds. Suddenly Lekan began shouting and gesturing because he was certain that he had seen a Papyrus Gonolek, a very rare bird indeed. This is considered a great omen of good fortune so Lekan urged them all to sit quietly, perhaps the beautiful red and yellow bird would reappear thereby insuring good fortune for the entire village. In just a few moments the bird returned, alighting softly on a limb directly above Lekan. They watched in amazement as the bird dropped a seed from an aloe vera plant on Lekan's head and then flew away. Unbelievable! Everyone knows that this is an act of incredibly good fortune, so they called off the hunt to hurry home and share the wonderful news with their village.

They were in such a rush that Lekan failed to pay attention to where he was going and stepped on a Puff Adder which bit him on the foot. His sons dispatched the snake, but the damage was done. They wailed in anguish; how could this happen after the good fortune foretold by the Papyrus Gonolek?

The boys hoisted their father in their arms. They ran as fast as they could, shouting for Imame the spiritual leader and noted healer who met them on the edge of the Village then directed them to his hut. Imame counseled the boys that the prognosis was not good, but he would try his best. He began with powerful incantations and an ancient chant to summon the ghost of Lekan's ancestors to aid him in his time of need. The healer progressed to bloodletting and then concocted a poultice of bark from the Pygeum tree mixed with grape leaves and fermented figs. He brewed tea from the bark of the Violet Tree and forced Lekan to drink it.

Imame invoked all of his considerable knowledge to save the beloved Elder of the community. He called on Lekan's wives and children to pray over him. They prayed to the spirits to cause the poison to fly out of his body. At times they thought that Lekan had died.

On the fourth day the worst was past and the community began to believe that he would recover. The Elder's held a conference and after much debate decided that something bad had occurred in the world as they knew it. The sighting of a Papyrus Gonolek was no longer a token of prosperity but had become just the opposite, a sign of imminent bad luck. The Elders caused runners to go forth to the other Villages to spread the word, women and children averted their eyes when flights of birds were in the vicinity and the lives of the villagers became oppressed.

And so it came to pass that Talib was sharing this story at the birth celebration of his nephew Zaire. All the Elders oohed and awed at the importance of this account, except for Jaheem who was the most revered of the Elders, his voice carried more weight than all of the others combined. Finally, he spoke, and everyone listened carefully to his proclamation, "Talib," he began in his sonorous baritone voice, "you must go back to Imame and Lekan and tell them that in most instances they have the wisdom of the Ancestors, but in this matter, they are as ignorant as the hind end of a Wildebeest."

The Leader's responded in amazement that Jaheem would insult such renowned dignitaries in this fashion. They muttered and argued among themselves for several minutes before Jaheem continued, "Think about it. For a thousand years the Papyrus Gonolek has been a symbol of good fortune and that fact has not changed. Here is what happened, Lekan's path through the forest was determined by the breath of the wind, the force of the earth, the influence of the moon and stars; he had no more choice in where he walked than did the snake who was predetermined to be where it was at the exact moment Lekan crossed its path. It was all fated at Lekan's birth, nothing could have changed it. However, a most fortunate thing happened just moments before this terrible snakebite. Lekan was marked by the supreme good blessing of one of our most important symbols of fortune. The Papyrus Gonolek is what saved him, otherwise he would be dead as we speak.

Jaheem sat back as the Elders absorbed this information. They discussed it among themselves and soon came to realize that Jaheem was speaking the truth; Talib was dispatched back to Lekan's village carrying the news to Imame and the rest of the community. They all rejoiced in amazement at the revelation of this most excellent edict restoring the Papyrus Gonolek to its rightful position as a revered symbol of good fortune.

However, that is not the end of the story. A year passed and another baby was born into the village and everyone came from miles around for the birth celebration. After the main festivities were observed, the Elders once again settled in for a discussion, "What news do you bring, Talib," Jaheem asked?

"Have you heard of the news from Lekan's village, Talib began? "Here is what happened. Do you remember the White Humans that came about two months ago?"

"Yes," replied Jaheem, "these fools came to the village and brought an image on a scroll that showed a baby in a feed trough just as you would use for feeding the donkeys. They attempted to make us believe that this baby was a God. 'If you get down on your knees to this baby God and worship it and bring it tribute then it will love you and provide you with nourishment of your body and love of your fellow man,' they told me. Well, I said, 'we already have all the love and nourishment that we need.'

I tried to be polite to them, but I wanted to say, you come here all pale and sagging barely able to make the trek from the river and you want us to give your Baby God tribute. I think the tribute was for the flabby humans; regardless, I sent them away with caution not to come back."

Talib nodded and gestured at this news, "Just as it should be. They came to our village and we did the same. When they got to Lekan and Imame's village, Imame attempted to shoo them away, just as you did, but they cornered Lekan and gave him much in the way of tribute, beads and a devise which would show your face like looking in a sunny lake. Then they gave Lekan some fermented grape juice which he drank and became more amenable to their baby God. They promised him they would give him more of this powerful drink if he would show them where he got the bright stones that we weave in the women's hair.

So Lekan agreed to do so and he took his youngest son. Along the way his son spotted a Papyrus Gonolek and Lekan began throwing rocks at the bird and shouting that it was a false God. He did this to impress the White Humans of his sincerity. His son tried and tried to make him stop but he would not. About this time another member of the party killed a monkey that got stuck in the tree. Lekan was so disoriented from the powerful drink that he went up the tree himself. Well, when he reached the uppermost branches that monkey jumped up screeching onto Lekan's face causing him to fall from the tree and break his neck and he was dead." Jaheem and the other elders nodded their agreement that this is as it should be. Ignoring a Papyrus Gonolek is one thing but to abuse it with rocks and bad language is sure fire death.

"What happened to the pale humans?" Jaheem asked.

"The last that was seen of them they were paddling, for all they were worth back downstream, but they forgot the image of the baby God so Imame put it on Lekan's hut as a reminder to all who choose to ignore the ancient paths of wisdom."

ACKNOWLEDGEMENTS

There are only six stories in this slim volume, out of the hundreds that I've written over the years. From my earliest memories, I can remember stringing letters together to form words and words to form sentences. I don't have to look far for who inspired me to put those thoughts on paper. My mother, Betty Lue, kept a journal. From an early age, I can remember her sitting at the kitchen table late at night recording the events and thoughts from the day. I still have those journals and I'll pass them on to my children. She wrote newsletters not just at Christmas but throughout the year. She inspired all of us to the written word and the thought process required to chain those words together. I want to acknowledge my brothers and sisters and my children, all of whom have helped along the way. A big debt of gratitude goes to my partners in Living Springs Publishers, My brother Dan and my sister Jacqueline, who have made the journey worthwhile by putting my words into print.

ABOUT THE AUTHOR

Henry Peavler can best be described as a writing junky. His four-part historical novel, Sam Wood, is three-fourths completed. He writes poems, which no one reads, fiction which a few people read and publishes a newspaper which a lot of people read. He has battled cancer for the last 20 years and, in spite of it all, he continues to write from his home in Mazatlán, Mexico.